BIG JACK is DEAD

Harvey Smith

BIG JACK IS DEAD

Harvey Smith

"Out of the crooked timber of humanity, no straight thing was ever made."

Immanuel Kant

"It's not what you're looking at that matters, it's what you see."

Henry David Thoreau

"There is nothing more depressing than trying to appear happy when you are not."

Nick Cave

PROLOGUE

I flew to Houston first class. Why not? Your dad only kills himself once. The seat next to me was empty, which was great since I didn't feel like talking to anyone. *So what brings you to Texas?*

Slumping back in the seat, I turned my head and pressed my cheek against the cool leather. The plane wobbled and dipped, rattling a tray nearby. Two men across the aisle stopped talking briefly and the seat belt reminder chimed and lit up. We jerked around then hit smooth air, leveling out. An airline attendant passed, offering blankets. I closed my eyes to erase the people around me, cupping a glass of ice in my left hand. The whiskey was gone, but the smell was still strong and the ice cubes still carried the flavor. I struggled to unwind even as the warmth of the drink spread through me.

It would be impossible to relax around my family. They would come up with stunts I couldn't predict, guided by unknowable winds that resulted in improbable acts.

The fingers of my free hand clambered along the length of the armrest, searching for the button to recline the seat. I mashed it down and pushed backward until the angle was better. My eyebrows came together as I worked on what felt like a puzzle or a trap devised by forces outside my influence. Lowfield was my hometown on the Gulf Coast. I was bound to my family and to the place of my birth by shared history, by the power they held as a starting point. I wanted to see my brother Brodie, but this desire usually got trashed in the first hour. Something always came up between us.

The plane was cold, but I refused to take one of the blankets; too many people touched those things every day. So I settled further into my jacket, pulling it tight around the t-shirt underneath, where an eagle was tearing a snake apart.

The flight attendant came over and leaned toward me. "Want another drink?" She pantomimed the words, more than speaking them. Her eyebrows lifted up into her bangs and her mouth made a perfect circle. Part den mother, part sorority girl.

"Yes."

She ducked into her cubbyhole and came out after a minute. As she turned and headed back to my seat, I watched her legs. She leaned forward with another drink and a cocktail napkin, flashing me a smile as she arranged it on the tray in front of me. I wondered about her panties and bra, deciding on black and thin. I pictured her bush waxed into a narrow strip.

A while later, I got up to pee, taking the glass with me. I made my way toward the washroom, squeezing past a girl who was no more than nineteen wearing designer pajamas.

Headphone cords dangled from her ears and our bodies brushed as I passed. We smiled awkwardly at one another.

Wedging myself into the washroom, I sat my drink down on the counter next to the soap pump. On a plane, it's amazing how relaxing it is to step into this small space, invisible to everyone else. Leaning forward, I stretched my back. Tightness fell away from me as I rested my hands on the counter. The overhead light lit my face with an otherworldly shade of aqua. I leaned closer to the mirror, close enough to see how bloodshot my eyes were. After splashing water over my face, I felt better for a moment, but then my thoughts leapt back to why I was on the plane. Funny how death keeps surprising you.

The drone of the plane went away and I saw my father sitting in a dark house. I could hear the wind moaning through the cracks. He was living on candy bars and crying, smelling like four-day-old shit and sucking on the cool metal of a gun barrel. He looked old and haggard, alone in the last minutes of his life. I picked up my glass and drained it.

At the office I hadn't told anyone why I was taking off. Near the end of the day I sent a vague message about a family situation. Mandy feigned concern and asked if I wanted her to come over *in case I wanted to talk*. I considered it, but declined the invitation. Leaving her to book the flight, I went to pack. Now I was drinking alone in a tiny toilet, 25,000 feet above the ground. After washing my face again, I traced my forehead, eyelids and neck with an ice cube. The floor vibrated under my feet as the plane shuddered and the engine sounds increased in pitch. Back at my seat I considered ordering another drink, but decided to sleep instead.

The Gulf Coast humidity hit me as soon as I stepped off the plane. Everything I was wearing felt heavier and clung tighter. It was an effect I never noticed while growing up. Relatives from out of state always mentioned it when they came down for the holidays. Now I understood. It was totally obvious to me after living in California for years and I wondered again how people managed to live down here.

I made my way out of the terminal and rented a Lexus with dark-tinted windows. Guiding the car through the dense market of airport traffic, I was out on the highway ten minutes later with the windows cracked and my bags resting beside me in the passenger seat.

Oddly, I started to feel good. In Sunnyvale, I always felt like I was under observation. Down here all that slid away. What did I have to prove to these people? A feeling of familiarity settled over me as I drove along. The world outside was flat, eaten up with strip malls and gas stations. The whole place was tied down by black telephone wires, like Gulliver. The ground was riddled with fire ant mounds, and you were almost guaranteed to find a wood roach tucked into every crack. Ditches filled with trash hemmed the highway and flat salt grass fields lay beyond. The contrast with the Bay Area was startling and yet somehow it all felt familiar.

I started to move the car into the left-hand lane, but a black truck sped up to prevent me from getting over. *Fuck.* I stepped on the gas and squeezed into the gap anyway, coming inches from hitting the truck. It all happened in a thin slice of flying road, the emotion and the movement. The driver of the truck drafted behind me, deliberately close, then swerved over into the far right lane and began passing cars, weaving in and out of traffic as he darted upstream. I maintained my speed, watching through the darkened glass and pressuring the sedan in front of me in a bid to stay ahead of the truck. It slid into place a few cars further on, accelerating and leaving me behind. Gritting my teeth, I imagined the driver laughing at me.

I saw his truck spin out of control, leaping into the air like a tortured, bucking animal. It came down sideways in the drainage canal flanking the highway. No one else stopped, but I got out and approached. The driver hung upside down from the seat belt, face purple and eyes bulging. He gasped for breath through a neck that was snapped and swelling with blood. I knelt down, placing one hand on the window frame, leaning close. He gurgled as he tried to speak, like a baby, like an animal in a trap, like a ninety-nine-year-old in a rest home bed. Tears formed in his eyes.

I felt my heart beating at a crazy pace as I drove. Someone honked twice, reacting to the maneuvering. I shook it off and tried to breathe again, my face hot and puffy. The drivers around me drifted apart, adjusting for space. I swallowed and ran my tongue over my teeth, slowing the car as I slid back into the middle lane.

Whenever I went home, I stayed at the El Cinco Inn, a chain motel common throughout the region. The rooms were small and smelled liked smoke. The walls sweated from the humidity and the carpet was so thin that when I walked barefoot I could feel the grooves in the concrete slab underneath. Huge roaches sometimes ran across the wallpaper in the middle of the night, skeptical blots from a disgusting Rorschach test. *What am I afraid of? Three-inch wood roaches crawling into my fucking mouth at night.*

The El Cinco was dismal, but there was no choice. I found myself near breaking after being with my family for even a few hours, ready to have a stroke or kill one of them slowly. The only relief was getting away. At the end of an evening, at least I could drive back to the motel, pull the filthy curtains closed and watch bad television in bed, with people above, below and to the sides like wasps curled up in paper-mâché nests.

Staying at the El Cinco involved turning down offers from both my mother, Ramona, and my stepmother, Mincy, the two women who had lived with my father for the longest period during my childhood. I always declined, mumbling about privacy or making a joke about picking up some local girl. Ramona reacted with a numb acceptance that angered me and disturbed me in equal parts. Mincy always made a fuss, playing disappointed and hurt.

The thought of them suffering through life with my father made me shudder. He was prone to infantile rage, occasional violence and an incessant demand for sex. Extreme jealousy and paranoia possessed him at random times. Socializing with him was nearly impossible. He hated our neighbors and avoided most gatherings, including parties and church. When he wasn't working, he was at home, where he usually sat around in his underwear listening to country music. He drank and never said anything that wasn't sarcastic or full of fury.

My father made very little money. (Or had, I reminded myself.) And he often wasted it, buying things outside his means on impulse. Coming home from work once, he stopped on the side of the road and bought a ski boat that wouldn't run. In high school, I saved up several hundred dollars in a college account. My father withdrew it and spent it on a thoroughbred horse that he sold a couple of years later.

Somehow, despite all this, these women managed to live with him for years. I wondered what they gained by living like that. Back in the Bay Area, Mandy made sense to me. She was ambitious, even as a personal assistant. As part of our unspoken arrangement, her salary was twice that of her peers, no one tracked her vacation time, and occasionally I fired someone she didn't like. Obviously, she didn't want to marry me. In exchange, all I had to do was reach for her.

I pulled into the El Cinco parking lot and shut off the engine. The emergency brake sounded like some kind of torture device tightening down. Gathering my bags, I walked to the motel office. One of the automated glass doors had been shattered and electrical tape ran outward from the central point of impact.

The lobby was Southwestern, but everything looked artificial. What's worse than a cow skull hanging on the wall? A plastic cow skull. This region was about as far from an O'Keeffe painting as Jupiter. Someone following a corporate decorating guide had positioned 3' tall jars of red peppers in all the corners. A television hung near the ceiling providing white noise.

Two women were working the counter. Both of them were obese, with rolls of fat bulging from under their El Cinco uniforms. Flush-faced, they seemed excited about something. The odor of cigarette smoke was almost overpowering. I relaxed, fighting against the contempt climbing up inside me.

"Hi," I said. "I just need a room for a few nights."

"Do you have a reservation?" Suddenly, the woman in front of me was all business. Her companion occupied herself by smoothing down the pleats of her uniform, pausing once to pluck the material from between two folds of her flesh with pudgy fingers.

"No," I said. "I didn't have time to make one…"

"Well, we've got some families coming in for a reunion. It might be hard…"

"My father just died. He killed himself."

A few seconds of silence passed. The El Cinco staff was stunned into submission faster than if I'd pulled a pistol on them. They stood behind the desk in their identical uniforms, the counter top a wide lake of reflective Formica. Finally, one of them made a quivering recovery. "I'm real sorry," she said. "We'll get you situated right away." She nodded in time with her words.

"Thank you," I said.

Chapter 1

1972

Jack walked home from elementary school, clutching a stack of construction paper drawings in one hand. His stomach rumbled, but he was in no hurry. Rain clouds gathered overhead and the wind picked up, blowing a paper cup down the street. He leaped out into the gutter to stomp it flat, his windbreaker spreading like a sail, the hood snapping out behind him as he landed. It was early in the afternoon and there was no one else on the street. The song from a distant snow cone truck warbled over the rooftops, off-key and half speed.

His house was at the end of the block. It was the second home he could remember. Built in the 1940's, an older relative once said, it was small with a handful of rooms. The exterior was white with mossy window frames that sloughed off paint chips like molting insects. Sitting on pier and beam-style blocks, the house concealed a dank underbelly that was thick with roaches and fat-bodied spiders, legs like black fishing line. His parents talked about moving, but for now this was home.

He slowed, spotting a familiar car parked on the street a few houses down. It was a rusted VW bug that belonged to Daryl, one of his mother's friends. When Jack's father wasn't home, his mother acted differently, especially around Daryl. She had special rules for those times, rules that Jack had to keep.

BIG JACK is DEAD

Putting his head down, he trudged through the clumps of clover in the front yard, following a path that allowed him to hit a couple of outgrowths. The toes of his sneakers turned green. A fire ant mound caught his attention, but he couldn't muster the enthusiasm to kick it to pieces. Using his body as a wedge, he forced himself between the screen and the front door. The spring on the screen door groaned as it stretched out against his back and shoulder. The front door was locked. Leaning into it with his weight, he rested there between the hard wood and the wire mesh, knocking as loudly as he could, which wasn't very loud. Using the flat of his hand, he slapped the door, trying to get his mother's attention.

When Ramona opened the door, Jack nearly tumbled over the threshold. She wore a blouse covered in cream-colored splotches, a pair of cutoffs and nothing else. Her red hair was cut closer than usual and was badly disheveled. She stepped aside, adjusting the shorts on her hips.

"Ohhh...come in, baby." With an air of dreaminess, she reached out, stroking his head with unsteady hands. Once he was inside, she locked the door.

Jack blinked in the dimness. "Mom, look."

"Yeah, baby...those are real good." She took the drawings and dropped them on the coffee table. "Sit down on the couch, okay?"

He did as she asked, wide blue eyes locked onto her as she turned on the television. Twenty years old, she was slender and pale. Her breasts were larger than her petite frame would otherwise suggest and hung low within the baby doll blouse.

"You wanna watch cartoons?"

Jack nodded as she found the right channel.

"Here you go. I'll give you a hug then I'm gonna be in the other room, alright?"

"Okay." He watched her approach. Ramona slid onto the couch next to him and he leaned into her clumsily, holding onto her shoulder with one pale hand. She hadn't showered today and he could smell her skin and her hair, a combination of cigarette smoke, day-old deodorant and sweat. The smell of his mother and the warmth of her flesh made him feel safe. Holding on, he buried his head in her blouse, pressing his face against her floppy breasts through the thin material. He closed his eyes and smiled.

Ramona took his shoulders and gently pushed him back. Looking down at him, she smiled back, distantly, before getting serious. "You 'member what we talked about?"

BIG JACK is DEAD

Daryl's voice came through the walls. "Hey, Ramona," he bellowed.

She looked over her shoulder toward the bedroom then locked eyes with Jack again. "Remember?"

He nodded.

"Okay, you stay in here and watch cartoons." She rose from the couch, pulling away from him.

He watched her recede, crossing the room quickly. The bedroom door closed and Jack turned his attention to the television. From the other side of the wall, Daryl said something but it was muffled. Music started to play.

Jack sat watching Speed Racer. It was shortly after one in the afternoon and he remembered his hunger. The television was up loud and the sounds of cars accelerating and exploding echoed off the walls. During a commercial break, he slid off the couch and made his way to the kitchen.

Rummaging around in the pantry, he found a loaf of bread, untwisting the tie with his small fingers. Standing in a kitchen chair, he slathered two slices of bread with a layer of margarine before dropping them into the toaster. He'd been told before to butter the bread only after toasting it, but with no one around this was a small rule that he generally broke. If he buttered it first, the bread tasted better, coming out of the toaster in a dozen shades of gold and lighting his

4

tongue up with the pleasures of grease, salt and burned things.

Big Jack, his father, had walked in on him once while he was toasting the already-buttered bread. Jack was sitting on the counter after a slow climb up from the tiled floor, aromatic smoke filling his senses. Watching the toaster greedily, he was barely aware that his father had entered the room.

Big Jack was short, probably five foot seven, with skinny arms and legs. A basketball-sized belly was molded to his lower abdomen and a pair of B-cup tits sagged from his chest. Intermittent patches of wiry hair covered his pale, freckled skin. Watching his son up on the counter, it had taken Big Jack a few seconds to realize what was going on. He looked dully at the toaster before his eyes flared with anger. "Boy!"

Jack jumped, his heels banging against the cabinet door.

"What're you doing? You want me to knock you through that wall?" Big Jack took a step closer. His eyes were red-rimmed from cigarette smoke and bulged in outrage. Standing in front of the counter, he stared straight into his son's eyes.

"No, sir," Jack said. He looked into his lap.

BIG JACK is DEAD

Big Jack held him with his gaze as the toast smoke rose next to them. When the toaster catapulted both pieces of bread up to the top of the twin slots, Big Jack took them immediately, holding them in the palm of his calloused hand with no regard for the heat. As a welder, his skin was impervious to the glowing tip of a cigarette. Hot toast didn't even register.

"Don't put this shit in there already buttered. You're gonna burn the fucking house down." Big Jack boomed down at his son, "Is that what you want? To kill us all?"

"No, sir," Jack said weakly.

"Now get down off the goddamn counter." Finished with the lesson, Big Jack left the kitchen and went out back.

Jack's stomach was in knots, but he relaxed as soon as his father walked away. He waited until the kitchen was quiet then pushed himself forward off the counter. Dropping to the floor, he misjudged the fall and scraped the small of his back on the way down. He twisted and moaned, crouching and rubbing his back. Letting out a sigh, he collected himself and started out of the kitchen.

As he passed the door to the back porch, Jack saw his father outside gobbling up the toast, finishing off each slice in only a few bites. Mouth stuffed with toast, Big Jack swiveled his head like a hostile, backyard blue jay. Unable to speak, he communicated with his face, furrowing his brow severely, scaring the boy into motion.

That had been months ago. Now Jack stood on a chair, mouth watering as he made toast in the middle of the afternoon. He watched wispy smoke rise up from the toaster and at that moment his father's battered black truck roared up into the driveway, home from work.

Panic ran through him as he remembered his mother. Hopping down from the chair, Jack raced through the living room. He reached the bedroom door and hammered against it with his hand. The music on the other side was louder now, reverberating through the house. Jack pushed against the door with both hands, palms splayed against the thin wood as he kicked with the rubber toe of his sneaker.

The door swung open, revealing his mother and Daryl in the bed a few feet away. Jack's mother was on her back and Daryl was on top of her. They were both under the covers, but Ramona's knees stuck out, framing his body. Daryl grunted and snorted out explosive breaths as his hips rose and fell, his face contorted with effort. As the doorknob hit the wall, Daryl and Ramona jolted, snapping their faces toward Jack. Daryl continued to thrust into the woman beneath him, causing the bed to shake and creak.

"Daddy's here," Jack whined, holding the doorframe.

BIG JACK is DEAD

Daryl's eyes popped wide with recognition. He flew up out of bed, sending the tattered quilt flying. His penis swung wildly, swiveling from his mass of pubic hair. In the same instant, Jack saw the pallid flesh of his mother's thighs, the ruddiness between her legs and the damp patch of hair beneath her bellybutton. Her breasts undulated like jellyfish hanging from her chest, soft and white.

In seconds, Daryl struggled into his jeans and scooped up the remainder of his clothing. Still naked, Ramona helped him out the sliding glass door leading into the back yard. Jack watched Daryl as he fled, hopping and hobbling around the wreckage of a collapsed shed. He disappeared behind an unkempt growth of aloe vera plants just as Jack's father slammed the truck door out front.

As soon as the sliding glass door was closed, Ramona slipped into her blouse and cutoffs with the agility of an escape artist. Still standing in the doorway, Jack's eyes were fixed on the puff of her hair as it vanished into her cutoffs.

Working the zipper with spidery fingers, Ramona hissed at him, "Go sit in the living room. Tell your daddy we was playin'."

He darted into the other room just as Big Jack tried the front door, cursing and fumbling with his keys. When the door opened, Big Jack struggled inside carrying his plastic lunch box in one hand, holding his keys and a cigarette in the other. The screen door snapped shut at his back. His first words were directed at Jack, standing in front of the coffee table. "Did you lock that fucking door?"

Jack shook his head. "No, sir."

Big Jack stood without moving in the doorway. He roared out his next question. "Ramona, why in the hell have you got this door locked?" His eyes were still pinned to Jack's.

Ramona stomped into the room, holding a cigarette in one hand and yelling back. "You want me to get raped by some Mexican or something while you ain't here?"

Big Jack smoldered at her across the room. He deliberated and reached a verdict. "No." At the coffee table, he dropped his lunch box and truck keys on top of Jack's drawings. He dumped a handful of change onto the table, one of the rituals he performed upon coming home. The coins rained down in a scattered pile that Jack knew never to touch.

Big Jack straightened up. "What the fuck is that smell?"

Jack stood paralyzed. Ramona tucked some of her tangled hair behind one ear, confused, but wary.

Big Jack took six steps in his tiny, nearly shredded work boots and was lost from sight around the kitchen doorway. "Boy, goddammit! What did I tell you about this toast?"

BIG JACK is DEAD

The words echoed through the house and Jack shrank into himself, cold terror rising in his chest.

After eating an early dinner and watching an hour of television, Big Jack stubbed out his cigarette, stood up and headed for the bedroom. A plate and an ashtray sat side by side next to his recliner. The plate was splattered with drying spaghetti sauce and the ashtray was so full that it formed a miniature mountain made of ash and butts.

As he passed Ramona, Big Jack said, "Come on. Let's take a little nap."

Jack sat on the living room floor running his Matchbox cars along the grooves in the oval rug. Quietly, he made small *vrooming* noises with his mouth, mimicking the shifting of gears. He stopped and cocked his head, listening to his parents in the bedroom, arguing. Jack froze, clutching his favorite car as the bed springs began to squeak.

After a short while, Big Jack came out of the bedroom in his softball uniform. He wore a team t-shirt bearing the Salvation Army logo, some stretchy pants and cleated athletic shoes. In the one-inch cleats, he walked as if he was a figure of towering proportions. They made a marching sound as he crossed the tile floor. The oval rug muffled the noise as he drew closer, dropping his gear and a pristine cap onto the couch.

"Goin' to play some ball, boy." Excited, he grinned down at his son with a competitive, almost maniacal grin. After tying his shoelaces, he took up the new cap, pulling it over his head snugly and looking down at his son. "Well, how do I look?"

Jack faced up, knees folded under him. "You look good. You look like a baseball player."

"Softball, remember? Baseball is for pussies who gotta get paid to play."

"Yes, sir," Jack said.

Big Jack studied his son for a second. "And little kids in Peewee League. Like you in a couple of years." Smiling uncomfortably, he reached out and pawed Jack's hair. "You're gonna whoop some ass someday like your daddy, right?"

"Right," Jack said, nodding and reaching out to touch the smooth aluminum bat leaning against the couch.

"I'll bet you're gonna make a good outfielder. Fast, with good eyes."

"Yeah," Jack said.

"Maybe we can play some catch this summer. You might be big enough now."

Jack picked up the crumbling leather glove his father had used since high school and held it out.

Big Jack took the glove, tucking it under one arm. "Alright. Is my cap on right?" Grinning, he knelt down a bit as Jack came close and tugged on the bill, straightening the cap.

"It looks A-okay."

"Alright, Daddy's gonna go win a game." Tapping the bat on the rug underfoot, he nodded to Jack. "You be good, boy. I'll see you later, before you go to bed."

Jack watched him as he snatched up his truck keys and walked out the door.

When the truck engine died away, Ramona came shuffling out of the bedroom, dragging now. Wearing nothing but a housecoat, she made her way through the living room, taking care to step over Jack's toys on the way.

He stood up a minute later and padded across the oval rug, carrying his favorite car in one hand. With just the two of them there, the house was quiet. In the kitchen, he hung onto the stove with his free hand.

Ramona stood at the sink, holding a cigarette and a plastic bag, smiling at him. "Hey, baby." Lifting the sandwich baggy, she exhaled into it. Jack could see her lips pucker through the plastic as the little bag puffed out. Lifting the cigarette to one side of the baggy, she burned a hole into it, inhaling the fumes deeply while it melted.

The smell of burning plastic crossed the room, cloying and unpleasant. She closed her eyes, holding the baggy and smoldering cigarette in place, repeating the process several times. The tip of the cigarette made twisting, expanding holes in the baggy. Finally, her hands fell, the bag slipping to the ground like a parachute shredded by hot shrapnel. She opened her eyes and smiled, groggy but happy.

"Come here, little Jack," she said. "Come here, my baby."

He crossed the room and continued walking until he collided with her body. Ramona rocked gently, settling back against the counter. Draping one hand over his shoulder, she lifted the other to her face, taking a drag on her cigarette. Ruffling his hair with a leaden motion, she exhaled smoke down around him, the soft cloud settling over him like goose feathers after a pillow fight.

Jack closed his eyes and buried his face against her belly where it was starting to swell with his little brother Brodie.

Chapter 2

1999

The last night of the conference, one of many for work, at a sidewalk restaurant with people I met earlier in the day. Sitting at the end of the table, eating and listening, knowing I would never see any of them again. The light in the sky falling through shades of blue, deepening toward the black eye of the trout lying dead on my plate, staring up at me.

A Tuscan place in a neighborhood where all the businesses are called firms. Indigo clouds, shot with five more minutes of silver. Watching the last pigeon of the day as it waddles between the tables, hustling for scraps. Everyone goes quiet when it hops up onto an empty deck chair in a portly act of athleticism. Laughter and another sip of mineral water.

After dinner, I walked several blocks to my car, the wind pushing bits of paper past me along the empty street. Dark trees punctuated the sidewalks in perfect rows, a circle of cobblestones around each tree. At a deserted intersection, the air was alive with the shrieking of birds. They dominated a tree near the corner, a screeching mob. I couldn't see anything within the leaves, but the sound was unrelenting, juggling bodies throwing themselves at one another through the branches. A dark shape flitted up out of the foliage into the night sky. Another dropped from the darkness overhead and was lost in the leaves.

Halfway across the intersection, I noticed the man on the park bench. He looked homeless, around fifty, though it was hard to tell. Mouth slack, eyes half-closed, body slouched back on the bench. A steady rain of bird shit fell down on him from the limbs overhead.

How do people end up being such disasters?

I stopped in the street, afraid, but wondering if I should do something. *I imagined him looking up quickly, lurching to his feet, running at me.* He stared ahead without moving. White clots fell down from the leaves, *plipping* from his shoulders into his lap, smearing as they streaked his jacket and got lost in his wiry hair and beard. Some of the shit hit his face, forcing him to blink, but otherwise he made no effort to move. The birds continued with their shrill cries and hidden movements.

Before looking away, I was struck by something. It took me a minute to figure out that beneath the beard and the filth he resembled my father. Roughly Dad's age and height, there was also something else, something about his expression. Pressing my lips together, I walked to the far sidewalk, heading to my car.

A couple of hours later I sat at a kitchen table with some friends. Jean and Micheline were putting me up during the conference. Micheline's sister, Clarisse, was also with us and another couple who were visiting from France.

I lifted my drink and rested the cool glass against my mouth, staring into the darkest corner of the room. In my thoughts, the birds still cackled and thrashed within the tree. I saw the homeless guy sitting on the bench and felt my stomach turn.

Conversations played out around me in broken English. Someone had thrown a lacy drop cloth down over the table, which was stained with the coffee, orange juice and cigarettes; years of familial tracks. Smoke churned in the air around us, slowly migrating toward an open window at one end of the room. Jean and Micheline had two kids who were sleeping in another part of the house. Earlier, I'd watched Micheline and Clarisse carry them off, lifting their little bodies from the couch and moving them slowly into the other room so as to avoid waking them. The kids slept through it, hair matted with sweat and limbs hanging limply.

HARVEY SMITH

Simon and Marie, the other couple, were smoking cigarettes. We'd gotten high earlier, but my buzz was gone. Partially-filled glasses of white wine and a few beer bottles stood clustered in the center of the table like a flooded city. I let out a sigh and rubbed at the scar cutting through my left brow...what a social worker once called "an act of adolescent curiosity, conspiring with adult negligence."

I'd driven up the coast to speak at a conference in Point Reyes. It still seemed strange that people paid me to talk about *social apps for creating team culture*. In my view, people just did what they did. They were born somewhere, grew up and took shelter; they felt happy, sad or angry; they fought, fucked and in general tried to get what they needed. That was the end of the story, the only speech the world would ever need. But traveling put everything else on hold and the conferences took me to interesting places. Two years before, in Hamburg, I stayed in a hotel that was an industrial cathedral. Every square inch was white or glass. The building itself was a work of art and had won some modern architecture award. It was situated down the street from a modern design museum and adjacent to a harbor full of tankers that seemed like a miracle of engineering, cleanliness and efficiency compared to the shipyards on the Gulf Coast, where I was raised. A company put me up there for a week in exchange for a one hour speech and a couple of interviews with the local media. I'd never been so comfortable; everything was sleek and clean and quiet. Sometimes I thought about that place as a way to relax.

Sitting at the table, I traded my attention between zoning out and studying Clarisse. She laughed a lot, leaning forward over the table every time she did, revealing the olive skin on her chest. She was attractive...fleshy, with cocoa eyes and lips that turned up in sharp corners.

"Are you sleepy?"

I shook my head. "No, I'm good."

"Li-ar."

I smiled. "Okay, maybe." We were talking quietly against the background noise of another conversation. Her English was good and it was impossible not to love her accent. Staying with Jean and Micheline, I'd been around Clarisse for several days, chatting, eating dinner and taking a couple of walks. Despite trying, we hadn't managed to get one another into bed. We came close once when the others went out and left us to watch their kids, who were something like four and five. Feeding them, Clarisse and I flirted and played around in the kitchen. Just as we started prepping for nap time, the younger child looked down at his plate, confused, and vomited all over the table. Before that instant, playing faux family was fun and we both seemed furtively aware that we would be fucking as quietly as possible while the children were napping. The vomit ruined all that.

The conversation at the table turned political and Jean and his friend Simon started to argue. Dull heat rose up through my chest, but I stayed quiet. Simon spoke in broken English for my benefit, ranting against some aspect of French government I didn't understand. Jean argued with him, sometimes lapsing into their native tongue.

While the two men were spitting at one another, I made eyes at Clarisse. Micheline and Marie looked bored. After a while, everyone fell quiet.

Clarisse's eyes darted to mine for an instant. "Uncomfortable silence is good compared to political bullshit."

"Oui," I said.

She laughed and everyone at the table relaxed.

Jean and Simon smoked and made small talk, giving themselves a break and trying to show that everything was all right. Simon rose after a while and drained his glass. He patted Jean on the back. After they said a few words to each other in French, Simon leaned close to me and shook my hand. He said goodbye in sing-song English and I couldn't help but notice that several of his teeth emerged at crazy planar angles. His breath struck me like the winds of Hell. I sat there, shaking his hand and smiling, but somehow his teeth brought back the smell of a rotting bird that I found under my house as a kid. My dad forced me to pick it up in my hand and carry it out to our garbage cans, which were wrapped in chicken wire to keep the raccoons and cats out.

Simon nodded and let me go, as Marie kissed the others and started collecting her things from the table. My stomach rolled because I couldn't help but visualize her tongue sliding into Simon's fetid mouth, past his tragic teeth. Everyone said goodbye for a while and then Simon and Marie left. Clarisse and I sat looking at one another across the table while Jean and Micheline cleaned up. They gathered up a bunch of glasses and bottles, carrying them into the kitchen.

I looked down at a spot on the table, studying a stain for a second before looking up at Clarisse. She smiled at me, coyly. With the others out of the room, I stood up and reached across the table for her hand. She took mine in a way that was clumsy and intimate, reminding me of elephants linking trunks on some nature show. Near the open window at the end of the room, I sat on the wide sill, leaning back against the stained oak jamb. There were no sounds coming from the kitchen; the house was quiet.

Pushing a potted plant into the corner of the window box, I made room for her and she sat down demurely, settling in opposite me and easing her shoulder against the other side of the window. We faced off in profile against the dark skyline beyond, with one of my legs drawn up.

I brushed the hair from her face. Her eyes and the tilt of her head told me that she approved. Leaning forward, we kissed softly in the light coming through the panes of filmy glass. Her mouth tasted like several good things at once... wine, lipstick and burnt flesh. We kissed harder and I closed my eyes while she probed the inside of my mouth blindly with her warm, wet tongue.

Chapter 3

1974

The alarm went off at 5AM on Christmas Eve. Big Jack lay comatose, unfazed by the buzzing. Ramona opened her eyes and blinked each one independently like some kind of white trash lizard. Sitting up slowly, she let the covers fall away from her nightgown and began shaking her husband in accordance with their morning ritual.

"Get up, Jack. You gotta go to work." Her mouth was dry and sticky. She paused, slipping into a daze and drifting toward sleep even though she was sitting up. Her eyes snapped open in alarm and she shook her head to regain clarity. She spoke again, louder. "Jack...get up, honey. It's five."

Big Jack groaned as Ramona continued to shake him. He cleared his throat and threw aside the covers, revealing his naked form. His arms and face had been sunburned a deep ruddy color, but the rest of his body was as pale as PVC pipe. He lay on his back with his belly flattened out like a vanilla pudding, rippling with his waking movements. Patches of very dark hair were scattered across his body. He sported a five-inch erection as hard as the tires on his truck and as pink as an eraser. Reaching down, he scratched his pubic mound.

It was still dark outside. The room was completely black because the windows were covered with aluminum foil. This allowed Big Jack to sleep through the day whenever he was pulling graveyard shifts at the plant. The window-mounted air conditioner kicked on, creating a lulling hum.

He reached over and took Ramona's wrist, pulling her toward him across his naked body. His eyes were still closed.

"Come on, Jack," she said. "Go get in the shower. We ain't got no time for this."

"It's Christmas Eve," he said. He mumbled the words so badly that it took her a second to make them out. He maintained his grip on her wrist, tugging her closer. The rest of his body was slack and relaxed, but his grip was unbreakable.

Ramona resisted for one final minute then let out an exasperated sigh. "Oh, all right, all right." She pulled her panties down and climbed on top of him with an angry commotion. The old bed was battered to the point of dilapidation and rolled under them like a raft.

Big Jack still hadn't opened his eyes. Once she was astride his body, he probed upward with his erect penis, blindly, making adjustments with tiny thrusting motions. She reached down and inserted it roughly, then began to ride him. It took four or five minutes for Big Jack to climax and he nearly fell asleep a couple of times. Moaning once, he barely increased the intensity of his bucking. Head tilted backward, his mouth hung open. As soon as his orgasm subsided, he relaxed completely and drifted back into sleep.

Ramona rolled away from him wordlessly, stepping down onto the carpet and making her way to the bathroom. When she returned, she stood by the bed and shook Big Jack firmly. Her eyes burned in the darkness.

"Get up," she said. She raised her voice. "*You're late for work.*"

His eyes jerked open and he sat up, fully awake. "Well, goddamn, woman...you want me to get fucking fired?" He looked up at her and shook his head violently to clear it. "What the fuck would you do then, huh?"

"I tried to wake you up at five, Jack. You're the one who wanted to do it."

Ignoring her, Big Jack slid across the bed and made his way to the shower. "Make some coffee," he said as he passed.

After showering, Big Jack dressed for work in less than five minutes. He wore the same jeans all week. They smelled like greased metal and were covered in industrial stains and burn marks. A thick welding shirt covered the t-shirt underneath. He owned half a dozen of the welding shirts. Each time one of them was too tattered to wear, Ramona went out and bought an identical replacement.

He sat at the kitchen table, drinking coffee and smoking as he gazed out the window. There were enormous goggles on top of his head and his work boots sat on the tiled floor next to him. His socks were peppered with holes. The window opened onto a small gap between the houses, so Big Jack mostly stared at his neighbor's aluminum siding. "I wish Daddy hadn't sold that place," he muttered.

Ramona stood at the counter making his lunch. She wore a housecoat over her nightie. Her slippers had once been fuzzy, but now had the texture of ratty cardboard because Ramona had stood in the driveway a few weeks earlier helping Big Jack start the truck during a rainstorm. She slathered a sandwich with the type of mayonnaise he loved, irritated by the burning sensation between her legs. The mayo was mixed with dill relish and chopped up bits of peppers. Big Jack called it dirty mayonnaise, which always confused his son.

The boy was sitting at the table eating cereal. Jack didn't have to be at school for hours. His parents' rutting had awakened him. He alternated between spooning cereal into his mouth and leaning forward to rest his head on the table, nearly asleep as he chewed. His father's smells drifted across the table, a combination of gritty Lava soap, cigarette smoke and strange odors from work.

"Don't fucking slurp, boy," Big Jack said absently. His eyes never left the gray dawn outside.

Jack sat upright. "Yes, sir." He continued to chew, but made an effort to do so more quietly.

"Goddamn…" Big Jack said the words casually, exhaling a cloud of smoke. "Ricky and I gotta weld galvanized today. You know what that means." He looked over at Ramona.

"Yeah," she said. "It means you gonna be hacking up your lungs tonight as we open up Christmas presents at your daddy and momma's house."

Big Jack nodded. His eyes rolled slightly upward as he considered the evening's gathering. He loved Christmas for reasons he could not explain and looked forward to all the associated events. With his tongue, he located and ejected a stray piece of tobacco that was stuck to his lower lip.

His mind turned back to work. "John-David got out of it," he said with a wide grin. "That son of a bitch is slicker than shit. He don't never have to weld galvanized. Any time we got to, he gets out of it somehow."

"Y'all oughta take turns," Ramona said. "It'd be more fair."

Big Jack looked confused. "Nah, it ain't like that. The foreman wants us all out there...it's just that John-David gets out of it, see?"

"No, I don't see," she said. She dropped a bumpy pickle into a plastic baggy and used a twist-tie to close it. She handled the pickle with disgust. "If they don't need but you and Ricky to get the job done, why can't it be just John-David and Ricky?"

"Ramona, please," he said.

But she was furious now, trembling. "That's how I see it. It ain't fair. I bet John-David ain't gonna be hacking up green shit tonight over the Christmas dinner..."

"Oh, goddammit!" Big Jack said, turning again to look out the window. "I can't never mention this kind of shit to you. You just ain't got no idea how the plant operates. And I ain't John-David." He smoked in tense silence then suddenly exploded across the table toward Jack, hitting him in the mouth with his open right hand. "Goddammit, don't slurp!"

Cereal sloshed across the room and hit the curtains. Jack was stunned for a second. His mouth opened wide and pink milk drained out. Then he began to wail.

BIG JACK is DEAD

Ramona flinched hard when Big Jack struck the boy. She rushed over to her son and held his face in her hands. She cradled his head, muffling his cries. "My god...what the fuck you gotta do that for?"

Big Jack bellowed, "I told him I was gonna knock him through that wall if he didn't stop that slurpin'!" He looked across the small table at his wife and son where they rocked back and forth over the boy's chair. "You don't stop cryin', I'm gonna give you something to cry about." He put one hand on his leather belt and the other touched the enormous, silver-plated buckle. The gesture brought to his mind the motions of a gunfighter, which pleased him. He relaxed, watching them huddled before him.

Shushed repeatedly by his mother, Jack stopped wailing and choked out cries only when the sobbing escaped his control. Finally, he was quiet. His eyes were red and wet with tears.

Big Jack stood up sharply and looked at the clock mounted in the stove. "Lord God... Now look what you done, boy. You most likely made me late for work." He looked down at his son. "You want Daddy to get fired? Huh? So you and your momma have to live out in the alley with the niggers?"

Jack sniffed and answered with his head bowed. "No, sir."

Big Jack crossed the kitchen. At the counter, he took everything Ramona had packed up and threw it into his lunch box, pouring the rest of the coffee into his thermos and closing the whole thing up. Grabbing his truck keys, he stepped into his boots before turning to his wife. "I'll try to be home early so we can have a good Christmas with Daddy and Momma."

Ramona looked up at him without speaking. Scowling, she held Jack, cooing to him from time to time. Back in the second bedroom, Brodie began to cry from behind the bars of his crib.

Big Jack stood still as he took it all in. His eyes bulged fiercely and he seemed confused. Whirling, he headed out the back door, flinging it closed behind him.

From outside, the truck door slammed and the roar of the revving engine flooded the kitchen. The tires made a sound like fabric ripping as Big Jack raced down the alley behind the house, slinging gravel and crushed oyster shells in his wake.

Chapter 4

1999

Back from the conference, I walked along the sidewalk in Sunnyvale, sticking to pools of shade from overhead awnings. Moving here from Texas, I never got used to layering clothes. In California, I was always sweating or shivering. I stepped off the curb and into the crosswalk at a four-way intersection. The road was paved with cobblestones for fifty feet along each street.

A gleaming convertible nosed through the intersection as I waited. The car looked like it was sheened in baby oil. Only somewhere below the polished surface was there any color, midnight blue flecked with silver. A woman sat behind the wheel, talking into a dangling earpiece. Her face was weathered and tanned, her body lean and athletic...a mid-forties face and a mid-twenties body. Off the top of my head, I knew that the car cost four times the money my father paid for the house we lived in when I was born, which made her more attractive. I envisioned fucking her from behind, kneeling in the passenger seat of the convertible.

A man and a woman walked along ahead of me, pushing an expensive-looking stroller. I marveled at them as I went past, even more impressed with the stroller. The thing looked like an off-road recon vehicle, with huge knobby tires and a web of straps that resembled climbing gear. Their baby rode along smoothly on the pram's complicated shock absorbers and suspension system. I wondered what his life would be like...organic foods from farmers' markets, trips to small islands, private schools, and a social environment filled with architects and CEO's.

The man must have been fifty, but was in better shape than I was in my early thirties. A phrase arose from somewhere...*twelve percent body fat.* There was a silhouetted figure on the woman's shirt in a yoga pose. Briefly, I saw the two of them fucking like actors on a porn set...smooth and tan, executing perfectly for exactly half an hour before coming in unison. My mind was awash with sex. Maybe there were too many beautiful people in Sunnyvale. Maybe the place itself was so manicured and health-conscious that it inspired lust and corruption.

I passed a restaurant and a boutique then turned into the courtyard of a small business park. Identical office windows hemmed me in on three sides, running up several stories. Workers clustered in the plaza or on narrow balconies above. A copse of trees stood near the center of the courtyard. All year long, their leaves were vivid purple, which never ceased to amuse me. No one else at the office seemed to think that purple trees were odd. I made my way over to one corner of the courtyard and entered my access code.

Our slogan was etched in glass: CONNECTING PEOPLE. As the doors slid open, the words split apart. Cool air closed in around me as I passed through the foyer and the magnetic lock *thucked* at my back. All the lights flickered on in the hallway ahead.

My office was small, dark except for the light coming through the courtyard window. The overhead fluorescent lights killed me, so I left the sensor off. Slumping into my chair, I let it twirl around once before flipping the lamp on. It blinked a few times and cast a cone of light up the wall. The monitor on my desk came to life as soon as I bumped the mouse. I responded to email messages for an hour, sending people documents, providing minor direction changes and in a couple of cases crafting small bits of text for the people on my team to use in various ways. My inbox was empty when I stood up.

I stretched, eyeing the clock in the corner of the desktop. My first meeting was about to start. My assistant Mandy appeared in the doorway just as I was about to leave the desk.

"Welcome back," she said.

"Hey." I looked up and smiled at her. She had curly hair, strawberry blonde and natural. It was tied up on her head with clips and a cloth wrap. Freckles ran across the pale skin of her face and breasts.

"I saw your message earlier and wanted to remind you about the proposal meeting."

"I'm ready to go," I said.

Walking down the hall, we passed an enormous window that looked out onto a street corner. Mandy said, "I just ground some coffee. It should be ready by now."

In the kitchen, I dumped cream and sugar into my mug. A young Hispanic woman cleaned the counter at our backs. Mandy took the mug and filled it with coffee. She handed it to me and passed me a spoon. I watched her move as I stirred.

"How was the conference?" she asked.

"Good, I guess. Pretty calm. I stayed with some friends."

She smiled and led the way out of the kitchen. "I've traveled with you. I know how you unwind."

"No, not this time. I just stayed longer because I needed a break. Nothing crazy."

"I bet."

BIG JACK is DEAD

We slept together despite her engagement, usually when traveling for work or after drinks at a company event, and she flirted with me whenever we were alone at the office. Being my assistant made it more exciting than it would have been otherwise. Her ass rocked from side to side as I followed her down the hallway.

Entering the room, I said hello to everyone. We were there to see two competing proposals for the front end of our new team-building software.

My phone vibrated against my thigh, so I set my coffee mug down and stood again. "Let me get this before we start."

In the hall outside, I dug out my phone, meandering into a small alcove made of glass bricks. According to the image, it was my stepmother, Mincy. I was glad I stepped outside before reaching for the phone. I never took calls from home in a room full of people. That was one of my rules...conceal my fucked up family at all times.

When I was a kid, Mincy had met my parents through her door-to-door cosmetics business. She and my father had gotten together after he threw my mother out one summer. Mincy was smiling in the phone portrait. While staying with her over Thanksgiving, I'd held the phone up to her face, snapping the photo while she bustled around in the kitchen.

She looked inexplicably happy, but equally confused. It was a signature expression…one that made her look like a middle-aged retarded woman at a daycare facility.

As I lifted the phone to my cheek, I could hear her sobbing. She was talking to someone in the background. "… well what did they say?" Her voice was distant, as if she were holding the phone to her shoulder. I pictured her standing in the kitchen, draped in the curly phone cord and talking to someone in the next room.

Anxiety came over me, spreading like liquid. It fell down from my face and into my chest. "Hello? Mom?"

"Oh, God…Jack. I don't know how to say it."

Fuck. "What is it?" I wanted out of this conversation already. It was difficult not to lash out at her.

She took a breath and sobbed before speaking, then the words rolled out in one short sentence. "Your father killed himself, Jack."

There was an empty delay and my head reeled as I tried to take it in. My chest felt pressurized and I steadied myself. She said something else—kept talking—but the words were just noise and made no sense. I opened my mouth to speak, but realized I was struggling just to breathe. It felt like someone was jamming a rolled up magazine down my throat, but I wanted to laugh at the same time. I can't explain it.

"I'm so sorry," Mincy said.

She and my father had been divorced for more than a decade, but somehow this had fallen to her.

"You know I always worried about this," she said. "You remember, I told you years ago I was worried about this."

Yeah, when was that? How old was I when you confided that fear? Middle school? I wanted to say something cruel, something to hurt her. I actually had the words on my tongue. *This is just what you've always wanted, isn't it?* I let the impulse slip away. "When did it happen?" I stumbled when I spoke and she couldn't understand me. "Come on, mom. When did it happen? When did he do it?"

She started sobbing again. "Apparently last night."

I bit the inside of my lip and rolled it around between my teeth. "He shot himself?" I knew the answer already, but she had trouble even uttering the word.

"Yes."

"At his place?"

"Yes. I didn't even know he'd moved. He was living in a house next to the river, in the old part of downtown."

Under my hand, the glass wall was cool and the air took on the quality of a hospital nurses' station. The alcove was quiet with the sedate terror of a place that routinely and bureaucratically managed death. *I'm afraid it's terminal...*

"Yeah," I said. "He moved a while back. He broke up with his girlfriend and went back home, to Lowfield."

"Oh, I bet she was a real winner." Suddenly all bitterness.

"I never met her." I leaned against the glass wall. "He was living next to the levee. Like the old house, but smaller."

"Well, this is just terrible, but I always worried about it. You remember how I always worried about it?"

"Yeah, Mom, I remember."

"Oh, Jack, it's so god-awful. They say that he wrote a bunch of hot checks and that he stopped going to work a few weeks ago...and you know how your daddy never missed a day of work." She continued to cry, leaving me silent and stunned. "He bought an expensive hunting dog and it was nearly starved to death when they found it in his back yard. You could see its ribs. They said it just whined and whined when they went over there. It was half-crazy and nearly dead. He just stopped taking care of everything." Her voice got shrill. "They say that he lived on candy bars for the last few weeks of his life. The place was just littered with trash...with candy bar wrappers. He'd lost so much weight. Someone said he was like a scarecrow, that his face looked like a skull."

"Fuck, okay," I said, cutting her off. "Okay, Mom." We were quiet before I spoke again. "I've got to get off the phone. I need to think. I'll be down there as soon as I can."

"Alright," she said, quietly. "I've talked to everyone else mostly. I'll try to reach a few more people later."

"Thanks for doing that."

"It's okay," she said.

"I'll see you soon." I hung up as soon as she said goodbye.

Standing in the alcove, I looked out at the world, refracted through the wall of glass bricks. I could make out the street and the leafiness of a tree set into the sidewalk. The leaves rippled like water behind the glass and cast shadows on the concrete. Someone passed, blurry, and cars glided by like colored fish. Looking down at the hardwood floor under my feet, I slipped the phone into my pocket and took a deep breath, swaying. The heat drained from my hands, leaving them clammy.

Of course he killed himself. Of course. Finally. Was there ever any doubt?

Thinking about the funeral made me close my eyes. *I saw myself walking along a buffet line in some church, pouring gasoline onto my family and my father's co-workers as they shuffled along the line holding paper plates.*

Head bent, I breathed out a few times slowly before making my way back to the conference room. Before opening the door, I pinched my nose and ran my hands over my face. Entering, I took a seat at one end of the table. "Sorry about that," I said. My voice was quieter than I intended, so I forced a smile at everyone. "Let's go."

Seated on the right, Mandy pushed my coffee cup closer, the band of her engagement ring clinking against the ceramic. It was still hot, but I took a deep drink, savoring the warmth, the sugar, the cream. Steam rose up into my eyes. I hid my face behind the mug.

"John, why don't you start," she said.

He started his presentation, cycling through slides projected onto the wall. Following along, I ticked off bullet points in my head, checking the proposal against what was required. Compartmentalize. Over a few minutes, I formed a conclusion. I asked a couple of framing questions as I listened, made a suggestion and provided some encouragement. As he was wrapping up, I asked a last question that very gently redirected one of his points. When it was over, I said only one word. "Excellent."

"Are you ready, Mathias?" Mandy smiled at the second man.

BIG JACK is DEAD

I took a sip of coffee and saw my father's face. He was *crying*. His eyes were bloodshot and he wore a stained t-shirt and a pair of jeans. His hair was wiry and streaked with gray. Wrinkles creased his face, many more than in years past. I saw him very clearly, as if watching him on television. Distended belly, diminutive frame and reddish skin on his face, neck and arms, a farmer's tan. Dad was sobbing and holding one of his nine millimeter pistols. The weeping was the most shocking part of the image. Everything else seemed natural, even the gun.

The words *I just don't know* formed in my mouth and my heart jumped because I almost spoke them, loudly and out of context. I clamped my jaws down tight and focused on the table in front of me. Control. I was halfway through the coffee and halfway through the meeting. I inhaled the steam and watched Mathias take over the mouse controlling the projector. I felt like screaming.

He launched into his presentation and I knew it was critically flawed from the onset. My hands started trembling so I wrapped them around the mug tighter and remained silent. I couldn't so much as nod.

Cued by my demeanor, the room grew uncomfortable. Mandy narrowed her eyes. Mathias grew nervous and mousy. He tried to make a joke, but no one responded and it fell flat. His expression changed...his every gesture and the tenor of his voice said that he felt like an asshole, but he had to keep going. He sat there faking enthusiasm, pretending not to notice the lack of warmth in the room. He hurried the last few slides and came to a close.

"Given the time line, we need to go with John's proposal," I said to Mandy. Everyone was quiet, waiting for me to say something more, but I couldn't. I put my hands down on the concrete tabletop and rose.

Mandy stood up next to me. "I've got all the notes."

John started to approach. "Good work," I said. "Integrate the feedback and get another version together as soon as you can." Walking out, I kept my head down and avoided eye contact.

Chapter 5

1974

Big Jack pulled up to his parents' house on the night of Christmas Eve. Ramona sat on the passenger seat holding Brodie in her lap. Jack sat between his parents. Nestled into a place where the seat had been ripped open, exposing the corn-colored foam beneath, he stroked the foam during the thirty-minute drive, savoring the texture. It reminded him of stuffed animals.

As soon as the engine died, Big Jack jumped down onto the driveway and slammed the door. Ramona and the boys clambered out from the passenger side. Rooting around in the bed of the truck, Big Jack tossed aside a paint-splattered canvas tarp and pulled up a garbage bag full of presents. Shifting his weight, he slung the bag up over his shoulder, where it rustled with his movements. He stopped at the edge of the driveway, coughed, and spat phlegm into the yard.

The entire family followed a stone path through the backyard. They crossed the patio, approaching the double doors that led into the house from the rear. A holiday wreath made of red plastic berries had been nailed to the lintel over the door. Tinsel hung along the jambs. Big Jack stepped up and opened the door. He didn't even have to duck to pass beneath the wreath. Stomping his boots against the patio doormat, he entered the den with the others following him.

"Well, Merry Christmas," Jack's great grandmother called out from the couch. The oldest living member of the family, she was diminutive and the hair on her head had turned impossibly white with no trace of color. Everyone called her Granny. "The kids are here," she called out to the rest of the house. Her eyes were alight and she grinned at them widely.

The house smelled of cloves and cinnamon. Candles burned and Christmas music from the 1950's drifted up from huge speakers sitting in the corners, hidden behind even larger potted plants. Most of the lights were off in favor of the warm illumination from the massive Christmas tree standing in one corner of the den.

Big Jack stood just inside the door. He stared as if thunderstruck. His mouth hung open and his eyes were wide with amazement as he took in the room and the Christmas tree. "Damn...look at all them presents. Y'all just gone all out this year, ain't that right?"

Jack's grandfather came out of the hall leading to the bathroom. "Yes-sir-ee, we sure did." Squaring off with Jack, the old man made a series of sparring gestures. He twisted his mouth into a feral grin and bent at the waist as he approached the boy. Stick thin, Grandpa pistoned his fists like a pugilist from another time, bringing his face down to Jack's and shouting, "How ya been, boy?"

Jack watched the gnarled hands moving in front of him. "Good, Grandpa."

His grandfather faked a couple of slow-moving punches then tweaked Jack's nose with force.

The pain surprised him and he almost sneezed, blinking and rubbing his nose against his palm.

"How's second grade?" his grandfather asked.

Jack looked at the floor.

Before he could speak, Big Jack answered for him. "Oh, you know, he's down there acting like a goddamn clown. Teacher calls about once a month to tell us about some shit he's pulled. Talking in class and not doing any homework. His grades is shit too. Ain't that right, boy?"

Jack continued to stare downward and everyone in the room watched him in silence.

His grandfather's smile vanished. "Well, son?"

Jack tried to speak, but wasn't sure what he should say.

"Look at him," Big Jack said. "He don't fuckin' care..." His father's voice carried so much disappointment and accusation that Jack's face began to burn.

"Now, here," said Granny. She spoke sharply and held up one of her delicate, knotted claws. "Let's not have any of that foolishness tonight. It's Christmas."

Big Jack peered at his son for a while longer before speaking. "Alright, Granny." He hollered into the kitchen. "Momma? Whatcha up to back there?"

Jack's grandmother called out from the other room. "Cooking, of course." She came motoring out of the kitchen wearing an apron and holding a wooden spoon in one of her powerful hands. She had a wide smile on her face, a smile that carried all the expectation of Christmas memories about to be formed. As much as Jack's grandfather was thin, his grandmother was stout, big of bone and wide of frame. She pushed into the room with a kind of power that caused the others to recoil. Jack called her Grandma and had always felt uncomfortable around her.

Standing out in the center of the floor, Grandma said, "Mother, taste this gravy. Is it salty enough?" She held the spoon up expectantly, ten feet from the couch.

Granny remained seated. Drawn up in her infirmity, she clutched at a shawl spread over her lap. "I can taste it, but you'll have to bring it over here, dear."

The two women faced off, mother and daughter. Neither of them moved.

"If it's gravy," Big Jack said, "it ain't never got enough salt."

"Ain't that right," Grandpa said, laughing with his son.

Grandma *harrumphed* and rolled her eyes back so far in her head that all traces of the iris and pupil were lost. She took a few steps and stuck the spoon out over the couch. Granny leaned forward delicately. She tilted her wrinkled face upward and tasted the tip of the spoon. The room grew quiet, save for Perry Como's crooning. Granny turned her head to one side, causing the soft, white curls of her hair to shift on her hunched shoulders. "Needs salt," she said.

Big Jack and Grandpa burst into a fit of cackles. Grandma snatched the spoon away and went back into kitchen.

"Goddamn, I need a smoke," Big Jack said. He dug around in one of his pockets, fishing out a lighter and a pack of cigarettes.

"I believe I'll join you," Grandpa said.

Big Jack dropped his garbage bag of presents and it slithered to the floor. "Put these under the tree, boy." As the two men went out onto the patio, Ramona set Brodie down and followed them.

Brodie wandered over toward the tree as Jack sorted through the presents. He picked up the first one, which his mother had wrapped in aluminum foil, and carried it toward the massive tree. Holding the gift, he looked up at the tree, a monolithic tangle of dark green and fairy light. Peering into the thick of it, Jack could see gnarled branches and the trunk deeper into the recesses of the tree.

"It sure is purty, ain't it," Granny said.

Jack looked back over his shoulder and smiled at her, nodding.

"Come sit with me."

He set the present on the velvet skirt under the tree along with the ones already piled there. Settling into his Granny's side, he scooted his butt around on the couch. She draped the shawl over him and hugged him. He looked back at the tree. The lights strung through its branches were mostly gold with a few strands of red here and there.

"What is it that Santy Claus is gonna bring you?" she asked.

Jack kicked his feet against the couch and grinned at her. "Granny, I don't know…it's supposed to be a surprise."

"Well, what did you ask for?"

He shrugged. "I don't know...maybe more cars. Some action figures."

She knitted her brow, the only dark hair on her body, and absently touched one of her snowy locks. After a second, she smiled at him. "You mean dolls, sugar."

He looked down at a frayed corner of the shawl that he was holding in both hands. "No, not dolls. They're super heroes."

Granny laughed and clapped her hands together. "Boys don't play with dolls," she said. "Of course. These days they play with these action figures. When I was a girl, Momma made us dolls out of extra buttons and old clothes we couldn't wear anymore." She hugged him and he laughed along with her. "You'd better get down and finish unloading those presents before your daddy gets back...but gimme a kiss first."

Jack looked up, studying her face. He gave her a wet peck on the cheek then bounced his bony butt a couple of times against the couch and sprang out onto the floor. In three steps, he was back at the bag, unloading it. Brodie toddled near and watched, peering down into the bag with curiosity.

The family ate until everyone was stuffed. They shuffled back into the den near the Christmas tree and seated themselves on the various couches and reclining chairs scattered around the room. Grandma placed dainty ceramic cups and saucers before each of them, save Jack and Brodie. She poured coffee for all the adults from a matching carafe then set out a pair of crystalline reindeer that held cream and sugar. Grandpa picked up one of the deer and tipped it forward over his cup, pouring cream from the deer's nose. He set it down and lifted a couple of sugar cubes from a hole in the other deer's back.

Granny was seated in the corner in a wooden rocking chair. "Are we gonna open presents now?"

"Momma," Grandma said, "...we will in a minute. Right now, we're having after-dinner coffee." She forced the thin line of her mouth into something that was almost a smile and spoke as if quoting. "This holiday season everyone is having after-dinner coffee instead of dessert."

Big Jack looked like a bird had flown out of her mouth. He stared at her slack-jawed. "We ain't havin' no pie?"

"Yes, dear," Grandma said. "But later..."

"...wouldn't be Christmas without some goddamn pecan pie," Big Jack grumbled, leaning back.

Everyone sat for a while, drinking coffee from the delicate cups. Perry Como's voice filled the dead space. "...follow them, follow them, you've been away too long. There is no

BIG JACK is DEAD

Christmas like a home Christmas, for that's the time of year...the time when all roads lead home." Big Jack drained his cup and got up to refill it. He walked over to a bookshelf near the record player, sipping coffee and looking at the old photos on display.

"That was my first gun," he said, mostly to himself.

Jack got up from where he was sprawled over a cushioned ottoman. He needed to pee and had been holding it since dinner. He crossed the living room on his way toward the hall, galloping with a skip-step like he was riding a horse. His grandfather reached out and snatched him up just as he passed.

"Come here, boy!" Grandpa pulled him into the recliner with arms that were absurdly thin, but strong from decades of driving nails. The old man tussled with Jack, hooting and flipping him around. He pinched the boy's skin where it was stretched over his ribcage, trying to tickle him.

Jack nearly lost control of his bladder. He made an *urk* sound as he writhed in Grandpa's lap, but otherwise went stone silent, struggling to keep from pissing in his pants. This, he knew, would ruin Christmas and signal his doom. "Please, Grandpa," he whined, "I've got to go to the bathroom."

The old man laughed and flipped him upside down. With gnarled hands, he attacked Jack's underarms, trying to tickle, but inflicting pain. Jack continued to beg and Grandpa laughed again, his voice hoarse as they wrestled. Everyone in the room watched.

About to wet his pants, Jack couldn't wait any longer. Desperation struck him and he wriggled harder. He and Grandpa went silent in their efforts, except for intermittent grunting. At that moment, the wiry old carpenter put an unbreakable hold on the boy and in an animal panic Jack sank his teeth into his grandfather's scrawny arm.

Grandpa released him and cried out. "Goddammit, boy!"

Jack sprang to the floor, bladder about to burst. "I gotta peee."

Grandpa swung his fist wide, throwing a roundhouse. Jack ducked the blow and Grandpa hit the wood paneling behind his chair, the impact booming through the room. A glass-framed portrait fell from the wall and exploded. Jack was wailing now and darted down the hall, unzipping his pants madly as he ran.

The old man bellowed from his position in the recliner. Contorting his spine, he threw his head over his shoulder and yelled, "You will not bite me, you little son of a bitch."

Everyone watched in stunned silence. Ramona blinked several times.

In the bathroom, Jack barely had time to slam and lock the door. He hopped like a wounded rabbit over to the toilet, tearing his jeans open along the way and unleashing a spray of urine that was not quite focused enough to be called a stream. He hit the wall, the floor and several spots on the commode itself. The roll of toilet paper hanging to the side of the bathroom cabinet was soaked before Jack finally got the entire operation under control and started peeing into the toilet bowl proper. Relief spread through him and he let out a bestial groan.

His grandfather's voice was muffled by the bathroom door as he yelled and cursed from down the hall.

When Jack finished, he zipped up and wiped his hands on his jeans. Mopping everything off with toilet paper, he cleaned up the bathroom as best he could. Then he stood in front of the mirror and looked at his reflection, chewing one small fingernail. Still winded from exertion, he heaved air in and out of his mouth. His breath whistled around his fingers. Finally, he opened the door and walked down the hall toward the den.

Jack could hear them talking over the Christmas music as he approached. To his surprise, they didn't seem angry.

Everyone got quiet when he entered the room. Ramona had already swept up the glass from the picture frame, leaving the busted remains of the portrait on a nearby counter. The picture was very old and depicted Jack's *great*-grandfather standing in front of a woodshed.

"Jack, come here," his grandfather said.

He walked up slowly and stood next to the recliner, head bowed.

Grandpa reached out slowly with one scarred hand and took Jack's shoulder. "Now, listen, boy. What you did was wrong, you understand?"

Jack nodded. Everyone in the room was quiet. Everyone watched them.

"I don't want you to bite any more, alright? Bitin' is for babies." The old man waited, looking at Jack through his black-framed glasses. "If you bite me again, your daddy is gonna whip you. You understand?"

Unable to prevent himself, the boy looked over at Big Jack who was now standing in front of the Christmas tree. He was silhouetted against the tree...a dark, empty body made of shadow and surrounded by glimmering red-gold light.

"Yes, sir," Jack said, looking back at the old man.

BIG JACK is DEAD

Grandpa tightened his grip on Jack's shoulder until the boy squirmed and the cartilage popped. "Are you sorry for what you done?"

"Yes, sir," Jack said.

From across the room, Granny said, "Now give your grandpa a hug and let's get on with Christmas."

Jack leaned forward into his grandfather's leathery embrace, smelling the strong aftershave around his neck intermingled with cigarette smoke. They released each other and Jack went over to the couch as quietly as possible. He sat down softly then bent over to re-tie his sneakers, which allowed him to disappear.

Big Jack turned to Grandma. "We gonna have pie now or we gonna open presents?"

"Presents first, dessert later," she said. "Ramona, set up a trash bag by the back door for the paper." Grandma waited until Ramona started moving. "Why don't you play Santa Claus this year, son?"

Big Jack's eyes widened. He turned to his father. "Daddy, is that okay? You don't mind if I do it, do you?"

Somehow this humiliated the old man, but he tried to hide his expression. "No, I do it every year, so you go ahead." Grandpa had always performed this function, choosing the presents to hand out and reading the name tags. From his seat on the recliner, he smiled meekly at his wife.

Big Jack stepped over to the Christmas tree and knelt. Everyone got settled behind him, taking up seats and waiting for him to offer up the first present. Digging around in the pile, he pulled out a small package wrapped in silvery-blue paper. He read the tag then set it back on the pile. After reading the tag on the next box, he turned to the room with a grin. "This one is to me from Momma and Daddy." He turned around and tore into the package. It was open in seconds and he tossed aside the thin paper, holding up a new pocketknife in a leather sheath.

"Hot damn," he said, opening up the knife. "It's a lock-blade." He got up and walked around the room, showing everyone the knife. It was ten inches long when opened, with a black and green rubber grip.

Jack saw his own face reflected in the blade as his father held it near.

"Look at that, boy," Big Jack crowed. "It's big, ain't it?"

Jack faked an expression of awe and nodded.

Grandpa got serious again. "Now we spent a lot on that so take care of it. It's a nice one...one of the most expensive knives they had at the gun shop." He grinned at his son.

Big Jack looked back at him and nodded. "I will, Daddy."

"Dear," Grandma said. "Why don't you pick out one present for everyone? That way we can stay on schedule." With a fingernail, she tapped the watch affixed to her thick wrist.

"Oh," Big Jack said. "Alright then." He snapped the knife closed and slipped it into his pocket. He picked out several presents, including another for himself, and distributed them around the room.

Jack sat on the couch opening an oblong package. He tore the paper slowly, afraid of appearing too greedy. He removed the paper and all the pieces of tape then folded everything up, taking it over to the plastic trash bag near the back door. Taking his place on the couch again, he opened the box carefully. It was surprisingly heavy. The lid came away, revealing a new BB gun, nested in tissue. Jack plucked off a bow and lifted the gun out of the box. All over the room, the others were opening their own packages.

"Would you look at that?" Big Jack said. "...I got a new thermos." He focused his attention on the object in his hands.

"Well, who was it from?" Ramona asked.

Big Jack blinked. "I don't know." He stared at her then dug around in the paper. He read the small tag and looked up at her again. "Oh..." He chuckled. "It's from you, Jack and the baby." Then the smile faded from his face. "Though you gotta admit...you, Jack and the baby don't work out at the plant. So I sorta paid for this myself." Ramona opened her mouth, but didn't speak. She turned her head toward the patio doors, staring into the dark backyard. Big Jack turned his attention back to the thermos and unscrewed the lid. He held it under his nose and sniffed for a long time. "Oh, man...I love that new thermos smell." He held it up to one eye, looking into the silvery glass barrel of the thing.

Granny called out to Jack. "Whatcha got, little Jackie?"

"A BB gun," he said. "I love it." He put on a smile.

Grandpa pointed at him and arched his eyebrows. "Now listen, boy. If I catch you shootin' anybody's mailbox or winders with that air rifle, or puttin' out some dog's eye, I'm gonna whip that ass. You hear?"

Jack pretended to study the gun in fascination. "Yes, sir," he said. "I won't."

Big Jack looked over at his son. "I had a .22 rifle when I was your age. Not an air rifle, but a real gun."

"He sure did," Grandpa said. "He grew up with guns. Not like kids today, with the television."

Jack looked up at each of them. He felt ashamed, but didn't know what to say, so he turned his attention back to the BB gun.

BIG JACK is DEAD

Big Jack gathered up another round of presents and passed them out. They repeated the ritual, opening gifts until the skirt under the tree was bare. With each round, Grandma asked Ramona to collect all the loose wrapping paper and stuff it down into the trash bag.

When all the presents were gone, Grandma lined everyone up for photos, directing them by pointing and shaking her heavy arms, making disgusted sounds and frowning until they understood her wishes.

Afterward, they ate pecan pie.

Chapter 6

1999

That morning at the El Cinco Motel, I woke up slowly, wondering where the hell I was. Finally, my daze passed. I remembered that I'd returned home and I remembered why.

Rolling over and kicking free of the covers, I sat in the near-dark at the edge of the bed. My shoulders and neck were stiff until I rolled them and stretched for a couple of minutes. A thin wall of light reached across my lap from a gap in the curtain, dividing the bed crossways. I blinked a few times and tried to wake up. My tongue felt swollen and dry as it moved around within my mouth. I rarely drank anything while I was visiting the coast. The water smelled even before it hit your lips and the coffee was thin and usually stale. I stayed dehydrated, surviving on the overly sweet orange juice they served in 24-hour breakfast places scattered along the highway.

The region had a distinctive smell, with the dank air acting as a carrier for various chemical odors. No one living down here ever noticed, but the smell assaulted me every time I came home. It went beyond smell. It was an atmosphere created by the gray landscape of refineries.

BIG JACK is DEAD

Waking up, eyes burning, it was always the first thing I noticed.

At the window, I pulled back the drapery, leaving the gauzy under-layer in place. Dust floated around me as the morning sun lit up the room. The carpet was stained and filthy even though it was probably vacuumed daily by the minimum wage housekeeping crew. My skin crawled as I looked out over the floor...pubic hair woven through the carpet fibers, interlaced with occasional roach legs or antennae. I wanted a shower.

In an effort to keep them off the floor, I'd draped my clothes over a chair the night before. I collected them up now and shook out my shirt and jeans. At the closet, I reached for a wooden hanger and the others went swinging wildly, clacking like dried bones.

The rectangular window over the tub allowed a fair amount of light into the room, so I left the overhead light off. With great care, I avoided the toilet's cold porcelain base as I maneuvered around in the tiny space. Under the shower, I started to feel better. The steam helped me breathe and the warm water woke me up.

My mind went to Mandy back in Sunnyvale, all red-blonde curls and petite body. She'd been talking about her upcoming honeymoon and this had a powerful affect over me. Eyes closed, I thought about taking her clothes off in my office, late in the evening. Pulling on myself until I was erect, I leaned into the cold tile and started jerking off. Pleasure rushed through me a couple of minutes later and I angled myself away from the wall, pumping semen onto the transparent shower curtain. The little spurts left clean places wherever they landed, clearing downward pathways on the filmy plastic before disappearing into the drain.

I coasted into one of the available parking spaces attached to my mother's government-subsidized apartment complex. The place was located in the far northeast corner of town, next to a massive field of salt grass. A train track ran alongside the road, throwing the place into a thunderous rumbling for short periods. The train served the numerous chemical plants in the area exclusively, freighting industrial materials into and out of the plants.

Horrible stories circulated about the contents of the trains when I was growing up. The words stenciled onto the sides of the cars were too long and too alien to pronounce. Over the years, a dozen train cars exploded, flooding entire neighborhoods with lethal gasses and forcing the evacuation of hundreds. Industrial accidents had killed three of my friends' parents. Once a field of cattle were found dead because a train passing through their pasture leaked chlorine gas. The entire herd suffocated in the middle of the night. Sometimes when I was trying to sleep, I could see them lying in the damp field, convulsing. I could hear them lowing and bellowing.

Not everything made in the plants was toxic, but that didn't seem to matter. Vacuum-sealed tanker cars often carried tons of small plastic pellets. These were shipped out to locations across the country and melted down for injection-mold operations. The pellets were compressed for shipping and a train car full of them ruptured during my sophomore year in high school, killing our quarterback's father. Tiny pieces of plastic. When the vacuum seal on one of the tankers cracked, the resultant explosion shredded the train car completely, tearing the man to pieces and showering the area with white pellets. Someone from school drove by and said it looked cool, like snow.

I switched off the Lexus and sat behind the wheel, looking at the complex through dark-tinted windows. It had been built by the US Department of Housing and Urban Development. All the people who lived there were ostensibly too old or otherwise incapable of making it on their own. The buildings were ugly, made of pale brick and the cheapest possible building materials. None of the structures had more than one story, giving the entire place a squat profile. Electrical and telephone wires crisscrossed overhead and occasionally something triggered a flight of marsh birds from one of the surrounding fields.

I glared out over the grounds, watching an old woman hobble from her unit to the central building, probably to check her mail. She wore slippers and a flower-printed dress, and there was a scarf tied around her head. I shook my head, wondering what she did every day, whether there were people who wanted to be around her, or whether she was just miserable and isolated, too broken to carry on a reasonable conversation.

Visiting my mother here for years, I knew that many of the residents weren't even old. Many of them were drug addicts who managed to hoodwink the bureaucracy operating the complex. Like my mother.

I locked the doors and walked across the parking lot. As I passed a dumpster, a younger guy approached me, very lean and ropey like a racing dog, wearing nothing but a loose pair of shorts and high top sneakers. He was so pale that an extensive network of veins showed from beneath his skin.

"Hey, want some smoke?"

"No, I'm all right. Thanks."

BIG JACK is DEAD

He seemed to forget about me, continuing along the sidewalk without response, rounding the corner of the closest building.

I walked up the path leading to my mother's front door. A strip of masking tape was stuck to the plate bearing the apartment number. The tape was peeling up at the edges and someone had pinned it in place with rusted thumbtacks. In faded script, the tape said RAMONA HICKMAN. A few potted plants were scattered across her porch, all dead. The porch light next to the door was covered with spider webs and the husks of moths. I reached out and rapped on the door.

A long while passed and there was no response. I knocked again, much louder. Finally, something rattled behind the door.

Muffled, but distinctly afraid, a woman's voice sounded out from the other side. "Who is it?"

"Mom, it's me."

"Who?" asked my mother.

"It's me…Jack."

"Jack?" She sounded confused.

"Mom, it's your son…Jack. Open the door."

There was a faint, "Oh." The chain clicked and rattled as she slid it out of the groove. The door swung inward, revealing my mother a few feet beyond the threshold, a shrunken figure in a housecoat. I smelled cigarette smoke and garbage. She was barefoot and her legs were covered with insect bites. Her kinky red hair had washed out to gray and her skin had an ashen quality.

"Oh, Jack," she said. "It's so turr'ble about your daddy." She just stood in place after speaking.

I wanted to turn away, to walk back to the car without a word. She would stand in the doorway for a minute, I imagined, confused and mumbling to herself. She'd close the door, go back to the kitchen, and smoke a cigarette. Ramona could not be touched by such a gesture. Her emotions, if she had any, were inaccessible. If I left and never contacted her again she would simply continue to live in the housing complex until her death. She only called me once or twice a year when she managed to get her hands on a phone or acquired a prepaid calling card. She only contacted me to ask for money, saying she'd gotten into a bind and needed cigarettes or toilet paper.

I let out my breath. "Yeah, Mom, it is…it's terrible. He was never happy."

"No," she said. "No, he wasn't." She looked off into space over my shoulder as if trying to remember something.

"Can I come in?"

"Yeah," she said.

I waited for another second and when she didn't move I took a step up into the apartment. My mother shuffled backward, allowing me to enter. She closed the door and hurried to lock it, awakened into action.

"Mom...it's okay. No one is out there. It's daylight outside and I'm here."

"Well, you never know about people," she said, twisting the bolt.

The place was just as it always had been before, maybe worse. There was a path cleared through the jumbled landscape of her belongings, leading from the front door to the living room, then from the living room to the kitchen. I knew that there was a single bedroom and a tiny bathroom in the rear of the unit. She'd piled every imaginable piece of domestic junk along the walls and most of the floor space. The place was filled with broken pieces of furniture, a couple of dead television sets, numerous trash bags full of old clothing, a barbecue pit that was missing its lid, a massive Christmas wreath on a tripod and a number of yard ornaments. The old TV sets looked massive compared to my new Sony.

I stepped closer to my mother, causing her to freeze. Leaning in carefully, I put one arm over her shoulder, hugging her. Her body felt strange to the touch, like it completely lacked muscle tissue.

"Oh," she said, recognizing the gesture. She smiled in a way that resembled a grimace and said, "Well..."

I made my way along the path to the kitchen without touching anything. Sitting down on one of the wooden captain's chairs there, I perched at the edge of the seat, avoiding contact with the ratty cushion tied to the slats in back. Every square inch of Ramona's dining table was covered with glasses, diet soda cans, ashtrays, food cartons, medicine bottles, celebrity gossip magazines, and equipment related to her books-on-tape setup. She'd acquired the ridiculous tape machine through a program dedicated to helping the blind. After that, being on a mailing list for the blind had opened the door to additional benefits.

She tottered through the dimly lit room, stopping next to her one working television. She picked up a pair of channel lock pliers from a tray next to the television. She fumbled with the pliers, using them to manipulate the controls. She twisted the broken-off knobs until the television came on and began to blare loudly. Holding the channel locks in her left hand, she straightened up and looked down at the screen. Long seconds passed before she moved again. Bending slowly from her thick waist, she went down again, trying to change the channel, but failing, the clumsy pliers slipping off the plastic knob.

"Durn it," she said quietly, repeating the process. Finally, she managed to grab the tip of the knob and changed the channel.

The frayed material of her housecoat blocked part of the screen, which was discolored and snowy. A male newscaster in his fifties was presenting a story on a local food drive. Waiting on my mother, I suddenly found myself thinking back to the night in Point Reyes when I watched the homeless man sitting in a torrent of bird shit. I could see his vacant expression, his lack of concern...the disarray of his clothing and the filth in his beard.

Satisfied, my mother returned the channel locks to the tray and rotated to look into the kitchen. Seeing me, she stood up straight, as if struck. "Oh," she said.

I wasn't sure what to say. Had she really forgotten that I was there? I exhaled deeply, trying to ignore the nasty smell in the air. There were three full trash bags sitting on the kitchen floor nearby. An apple core and an empty can of deviled meat had fallen out of one of the bags.

"Mom, come sit down. Please. I came to see you."

"What?" she asked. She stood in front of the television slightly stooped.

"I came to see you," I said louder. "To visit…"

"Oh."

I started to speak again, louder, but she shambled into the room.

My mother was fifteen when I was born, which meant she was now forty-seven. In Sunnyvale, I routinely saw fifty-year-olds jogging on the hike and bike trails or emerging from yoga classes, bouncing down the gym steps as they migrated toward their teardrop SUVs or convertibles. By way of contrast, Ramona had the body of a woman in her sixties.

She reached the table and collected her cigarettes and lighter from where they rested near a pile of cassette tapes labeled in oversized fonts. Settling into one of the chairs with a creak, she lit up a cigarette and took a long pull. Her eyes squinted into crow's feet. She exhaled a gout of smoke and coughed a few times. She tried to spit a small piece of tobacco off the tip of her liver-colored tongue.

There was a tiny pricking sensation against the inside of my wrist. Looking down, I saw a flea. The dark, aerodynamic body stood out against my skin. I reached over and took it between my thumb and forefinger, rolling it until it was crushed into debris. My mother didn't own a pet.

BIG JACK is DEAD

I stared at the window, trying to block out the sound from the television, trying to calm myself against the onslaught of this environment. Delicate lace curtains bordered the window frame, stained from years of smoke. The glass in every window of the apartment was completely covered in aluminum foil. Tiny points of light shone through tears in the foil. I never understood why old people in the area did this. Apparently it made sense to my mother.

"Mom, I came to talk to you about Dad. About Big Jack."

"Yeah," she said slowly, nodding. "Yeah." She looked up at me with a sudden intensity that surprised me. She held my gaze and said, "It's so turr'ble about your daddy."

I felt my chest go slack and I sagged forward, resting my forehead in my hand. "Yeah," I said. "Yeah, it is."

She went back to smoking and a few minutes passed.

I looked at the floor for a long time. "Who told you about it?"

"What?" My mother looked at me as she held the cigarette up to her mouth, her fingers crabbed around the filter. "Oh...your step-momma told me." She nodded, bobbing her chin a few times. "Yeah, she did. She told me... He never was happy, was he?"

"No, Mom. I don't think so."

"Yeah. He was a hard man to live with...a hard man."

More than anything, I wanted to be out of the apartment. I wanted to jump to my feet, push my mother's chair backward, and crash through the aluminum-foil-covered window.

I saw her flipped over in the chair, still smoking calmly, with her red-gray seaweed hair spilling across the tiled kitchen floor around her head.

Instead, I asked, "Do you have a ride to the funeral? I wanted to make sure."

Ramona nodded. "Yeah...your brother is gonna come get me."

"Okay, good." I stood up. "That's good. I'm going to see him later today."

"I'm glad," she said. "He's your brother. He's become a fine man. And handsome too." She smiled and I saw that her teeth had mostly crumbled away. They looked like raisins hanging from her pale gums.

I willed myself to go numb and tried to smile. "I've got to take off."

"Okay," she said. Her tone was flat. "Okay...let me get up." She rose weakly and I wondered if she was faking. She spent so many years trying to appear sick or beaten down, first in order to fool Big Jack then the county welfare agents. I had no idea what her physical health was actually like.

Maybe what was originally an act was now real, after living like this for so long.

She followed me across the living room, taking several drags on her cigarette along the way. At the door, I turned the handle and gave her another awkward hug, which felt like hugging a dirty floor mop in a dress.

The door caught on the chain and I nearly yanked it off the hinges in aggravation. I wanted to yell, *What the fuck are you afraid of?* Instead I looked at her, still very close. "Okay, Mom. I'll see you soon. At the funeral." The words made my tongue feel heavy.

"Alrighty then," she said quietly. The smell of cigarette smoke was strong around her, clinging to her like an atmosphere. She craned her neck a little and looked up at me more directly, her eyes larval and glistening. Her voice fell to a whisper, as if ashamed. "How do you think they're gonna do it?"

I swallowed. What the fuck now? When I waited, she didn't follow up. "How will they do what, Mom?"

She peered at me with new life in her face, more lucid. "You know...lay him out. How do you think they're gonna do it?" She peered up at me, rodent-like, seeming even older.

I waited, soaking in her words, trying to comprehend her meaning.

"How are they gonna cover up his head?" she asked.

"Ah..." My tongue roved slowly across the enamel of my teeth. "I'm sure they've got something, Mom. I'm sure they deal with this all the time."

"Will they use a bag over his head?" There was a childlike quality to her question and she pressed closer. She struggled with the concept, fixated.

"Yes. Or a veil." I stepped backward through the door, stumbling. My foot settled reassuringly onto the concrete porch as I stepped farther away from her. "They'll probably use a veil. That's what I've heard."

My mother looked down into space roughly at my midriff. Her face lost the odd intensity and went slack again. "Oh."

"I'm going," I said. "I'll see you at the funeral."

"Okay, then...bye." Her voice rose in pitch on the last word as she tried to muster her emotions for the farewell.

"Bye, Mom. Love you." I backed away another few feet then turned for the parking lot.

Chapter 7

1975

The snow cone vendor leaned down from the window of his van to hand Jack a coconut snow cone. As he smiled, the man's lips peeled back and revealed a nest of greasy, blackened teeth. Measured from the floor of the van, he stood about five feet in height and was nearly as wide. Jack reached up to take the snow cone, but his eyes were locked on the man's swampy mouth. Desire for the sweetened ice fought with disgust. Carnival music played from speakers mounted to the top of the van. The music had a slurred, metallic quality because the same song played all day long, several days a week. Whenever Jack heard the song, sometimes from blocks away, snow cones and rotten teeth came to mind.

Jack's mother carried his little brother Brodie on her hip like a sack of potatoes, shifting him to the opposite side so she could move her cigarette to the other hand. She waited as Jack finished at the snow cone van. When he turned back toward her, she said, "Come on," and walked away.

He bit into the ice and trailed along in her cigarette smoke, following her closely. The van pulled away and Jack listened to the music fade behind them. It was Friday, just after school, and Jack was happy to be with his mother.

Halfway across the street, someone yelled, "Hey! Ramona!"

Jack's mother turned around, shifting Brodie again. Twenty-two, she was slim and pale, wearing a flowered blouse and a pair of shorts. She was barefoot.

Mr. Bornado was coming across his front yard. He was over forty, but glowed with unnatural health. His hair was cut very short, making his neck look bullish. His skin was so deeply burned from working out in the sun that it was the color of an old football. He wore only a pair of frayed cut-offs, hanging under his beer gut like tribal rags. A fleshy splash of scar ran up his chest and over his shoulder like melted wax. All the kids on the block said it was from machine-gun fire, dating back to Korea. Mr. Bornado smiled at Jack's mother, revealing a wide gap between his front teeth. She stood in place in the street, waiting for him to close the distance. Though he was stocky, his body rippled with muscle just beneath a layer of fat.

"Hey, how are you doin'?"

"Fine," she said.

"You got your boys out gettin' snow cones."

"Yeah." She smiled at him and took a drag.

BIG JACK is DEAD

They all stood in the middle of the street under the sun, surrounded by a naked sky. As a station wagon approached, Mr. Bornado pulled Ramona over to his side of the street, drawing her along gently by her elbow. She allowed herself to be led as if the gesture was an act of chivalry. They continued to make small talk on the sidewalk in front of Mr. Bornado's house. At times they spoke softly in their gossip voices, which caused Jack to perk up his ears without appearing to pay attention.

Ramona put Brodie down on the cement after a while. "Take your little brother back to the house," she said.

Jack was still working on the last of the snow cone. His mouth was stained blue. Taking Brodie by the hand, he waited for a truck to pass then led him across the street. Negotiating a path around a pile of dog shit, the boys looked back across the street at their mother. She and Mr. Bornado were laughing. Jack stepped up onto the brick stair and forced his way into the house, struggling with the weight of the front door. Brodie followed.

A blanket of chilled air engulfed them. The air conditioner ran nearly twenty-four hours a day during the summer, keeping the house uncomfortably cool. Jack turned to close the front door, but his father's voice came from somewhere in the darkness of the living room.

"Hey, boy."

Startled, Jack turned to face the room. He blinked a few times.

"What's your momma and Mr. Bornado talking about?"

Jack's eyes began to adjust. "I don't know." He could see his father in the corner of the room, behind a tan recliner that was patched liberally with duct tape. The tape was so worn that it curled at the edges. Big Jack forced an opening in the Venetian blinds and watched through the small gap. He was wearing a t-shirt and a decaying pair of underwear. There were white socks on his tiny feet and Jack could see the entire heel of his father's right foot through a huge hole in one of the socks. Veins climbed up his father's Achilles tendon like vines and the heel was covered in calluses.

His father cut his head over and tilted it, bird-like. "You don't know?"

Jack didn't understand why, but something about the intonation, the inflection, implied that he should feel ashamed for not knowing. "No, sir," he said softly. He made his voice more like his younger brother's. Standing next to Jack by the front door, Brodie ignored the conversation. He began scratching and probing his butt with his little fingers, chasing some itch deep in his crack.

"Come here."

BIG JACK is DEAD

Jack walked over and stood a few feet away.

"Come *here.*"

When he was a foot away, his father leaned down very close, still standing in the corner behind the recliner.

"What the fuck was they saying?" asked Big Jack. "Are you deaf?"

"No, sir."

"Then what?!"

"I don't remember." Jack looked at the carpet. He tried to withdraw without moving, to cease to exist.

"Goddamn it." Big Jack turned his attention back to the window.

When it seemed safe, Jack backed across the living room floor in silence, moving toward his room.

"Shut the goddamn door, boy. AC's gettin' out." Big Jack continued to watch the street through the blinds, mumbling. "I ain't payin' to keep the whole fucking block in cold air."

Jack went over and shouldered the door closed. He sensed that his father was fully distracted, his voice no longer carrying any menace. The boy drifted through the room and into the hallway beyond, sinking his toes into the thick carpet. Sucking the last of the snow cone juice from his fingers, he relished the hint of coconut and sugar.

Jack sat on his bed with a pile of Hot Wheels cars situated out in front of him. All his games involved intricate stories; each car represented a driver with a distinct personality. He acted out the conversations between the drivers, pushing the cars across the crazy terrain created by the undulations of the blanket on his bed. In his hands, each car was capable of amazing, Speed Racer-style jumps. Each car crashed and exploded a hundred times a month, only to be reborn again from the flames.

He heard his mother screaming at his father in another part of the house. For the fourth or fifth time, a pan crashed as she hurled it across the kitchen in impotent fury. She stood at the stove while Big Jack sat at the table, interrogating her. Occasionally Ramona threw a plastic bowl or spatula, but she was always absolutely careful to avoid hitting her husband.

Jack played with his cars and tuned the noise out. Brodie was lying on the floor, manipulating a Speak-N-Spell, with its ironic name in yellow letters. The phone rang and their parents got quiet; the phone always cowed them. The entire house went silent except for the phone. Someone picked it up on the third ring. Jack heard his mother's voice, which didn't surprise him. Big Jack never answered the phone if he could help it.

BIG JACK is DEAD

"This is Ramona Hickman. Yeah, uh-huh...that's right."

Seconds later, Jack forgot about the call altogether. He shuffled backward on the bed, putting his back to the wall and continued with the cars, speaking for each driver with a special voice, mimicked from cartoons and TV shows. After a time, his mother called from the kitchen. "Boys...time to eat."

Jack and Brodie made a crazed run for the kitchen, which was part of their dinnertime ritual. They both jumped up at once and scrambled like a pack of wild pigs, knocking each other around as they raced out of the room, over various pieces of furniture and through the house. Jack beat his younger brother to the doorframe and shouldered him aside. They tore across the carpet of the living room and slid into the kitchen, gliding across the linoleum in their socks.

Big Jack brought the game to an end. "Go wash your hands and quit being cute. I'm not in any goddamn mood for this shit." His voice carried an edge. Both kids stopped dead and retreated to the bathroom to wash up, heads down.

Back in the kitchen, Jack sat down against one wall with the window to his left. His father sat at the head of the small table, facing the window, and Brodie sat in front of the window, opposite his father. Jack's mother placed all the food on the table and sat down across from him at her husband's right hand, with her back to the kitchen. Big Jack bowed his head once everyone was seated. The entire family sat in silence. No one ever actually prayed, but when Big Jack thought enough time had passed, he opened his eyes and reached for the nearest platter of food. This was the signal that told everyone else it was okay to move again.

Jack was always ravenous and the food smelled good. Eight fried pork chops were piled on a plate at the center of the table. Beneath them, a stack of folded paper towels soaked up grease. Loaded with butter and salt, an enormous bowl of mashed potatoes sat next to the meat. Closest to Jack, there was a Tupperware bowl filled with dark gravy. A straw basket containing a mound of hot biscuits was shrouded by a dishtowel. Lastly, a small bowl of Del Monte canned spinach sat near one end of the table near Brodie. The kids both dipped out a small helping of spinach at their mother's insistence and heaped their plates with the other foods.

Just as Jack was about to take his first bite, his father interrupted. Chewing, he said the words slowly. "Well, boy...your teacher just called and talked to your momma for a while. She says you've been up there at the school acting like a little son of a bitch."

Jack felt his guts go cold. He lifted his fork, but let it fall. He gazed down at his food.

"Not now," Ramona said softly.

"Why not? He don't give a fuck...look at him." When Jack closed his eyes, his father shouted at him, "Look at me!"

Jack looked up sharply, unsure of how to act. To make eye contact with his father usually invited further hostility, but he could not ignore the command.

"I don't know why you can't go down there, sit in your fucking chair and keep your goddamn mouth shut instead of cutting up and acting fucking cute all the time."

Jack looked down at his food again. "Yes, sir," he said. Brodie ate quietly, studying him with glassy blue eyes.

"After dinner," Big Jack said, "I want you to go into my closet and get down a belt."

A long thin whimper escaped from Jack's mouth. "Noooo." The boy said it so quietly that the words could barely be heard.

"Don't fucking whine!" His father fixed him with a hard glare, scrutinizing Jack with one eye cocked open wider than the other. "Do not fucking cry at my table. Eat your goddamn dinner." Big Jack was done talking and dug into another pork chop, cutting off a quarter of it with his fork then stuffing the meat into his mouth.

Jack ate slowly, picking at his food. His skin was cold and his stomach was sick. He felt like curling into a ball, but continued to eat, forcing the food down.

Without warning, his mother hissed at him, "Eat some spinach." He flinched as he looked up at her.

Big Jack didn't mess around. He sliced up the remainder of his pork chops into double-sized bites and poured some ketchup out onto his plate. He went through six biscuits, a cup of gravy, three pork chops and three helpings of mashed potatoes. Several times, he covered the entire meal with blizzards of salt, re-applying more gravy and salt once he'd eaten away the top layer. He used his fork like a weapon, spearing a couple of triangular wedges of pork chop at once, dunking the meat into the thick pool of ketchup then angling the entire mass into his wide-open mouth, rotating it until it fit.

When his food was gone, Jack stood up. Everyone else watched him in silence. His father and mother smoked. His stomach cramped as he walked to their bedroom. In the closet, he took down a belt with the word JACK etched into the leather. Crying softly, he draped the belt over the foot of the bed and bent over the ratty, queen-sized mattress. He buried his face in the cigarette-burned blanket. Fumbling with his hands underneath him, he worked his pants and underwear down to his knees and waited.

Big Jack came into the room after a short time. He took up the belt and started whipping his son. Jack screamed down into the covers, begging his father to stop. Big Jack held the buckle in one hand and lashed the belt at its full length across his son's buttocks and thighs. Twisting his neck, Jack looked back, begging. His father was reflected in the headboard mirror, face contorted with rage.

After an endless time, Ramona came flying into the room, howling like a wild thing, face wet with tears. "That's enough! Goddammit, that's enough!"

Big Jack stopped the whipping. He glared at her and when he spoke, he was breathless from the exertion. "Go to your goddamn room, boy."

Jack fled. Lying on his bed, he screamed into his pillow. Brodie joined him. Standing next to the bed, he tried to take his older brother's hand. Jack yanked it away and rolled over to face the wall. His backside and thighs radiated warmth. The smell of old urine rose up from his sheets.

The door to Big Jack and Ramona's bedroom clicked shut and a moment later their bed springs began to squeak and crunch with machine-like rhythm.

Chapter 8

1999

Around one in the afternoon, I drove along a stretch of highway running through Quailbury, where my stepmother Mincy lived. I stopped at a traffic light every quarter mile or so. Each intersection was surrounded by fast food restaurants, gas stations and parking lots giving way to recessed shopping centers. And wires...no matter which way I turned my head, I was looking up through a skein of cables.

Waiting for the light to change, I watched a kid hang plastic letters on the back-lit sign standing next to a chicken place. A dozen blackbirds oversaw the operation from a telephone wire on the east side of the highway. There was a drive-through liquor store next door. The sign at the fast food restaurant read, ALL YOU CAN EAT CHICK'N-CHUNKS.

Local legend said that the chain was owned by a wealthy Gulf Coast family. The old man was a little crazy and still made surprise visits to all the restaurants, sneaking in disguised as a customer. He had fired dozens of people for minor infractions over the years. I imagined pimply teens, wide-eyed and recoiling from the old man across the counter as he transformed from doddering customer to screaming executive founder. The old man once dropped his act and gave some assistant manager a new car for exemplary customer service.

Using a rubber suction cup at the end of a long pole, the kid slapped the ground with the cup, grabbing another letter and lifting it into the air. Twelve feet up, the plastic letter popped free from the rubber cup and raced down at him like a roof shingle in a tornado, a playing card hurled by some malevolent god. The kid dodged, hanging onto the aluminum pole like a lance, a stick-figure knight. A giant rooster eyed him from the top of the sign. "Hang in there," I said under my breath.

My light turned green and I started to roll forward, but a truck flew through the intersection going fifty. Mother-fucker. I let my heart rate drop to normal before pulling away from the light.

All the nearby towns existed in a sort of cultural fiefdom, united by their dependence on shrimping and petroleum. Each town played a role in the social hierarchy. The poorest people lived in Lowfield, where I was born. Those better off, but who favored living around pasture land and the ridiculous trappings of so-called country life, lived in

Quailbury, where Mincy lived. The people who managed the chemical plants and owned the local businesses lived in Uncle's Lake, considered the cultural high note of the county.

To my eyes, these differences were illusions, even if the people here pretended otherwise. In truth, everything in the region served to keep the petrochem plants running. Sometimes I wanted a hurricane to wash it all away.

I pulled into the Gravy Barn to meet my brother Brodie.

Stepping into the air-conditioned chill, I took in the smell of grease and cigarette smoke. I made my way past the families standing in the buffet line, and walked to the back of the restaurant. I found a booth, but it was adjacent to the smoking section…something I never worried about back in California. Cigarette smoke gave me a headache or made me sick to my stomach.

Across the restaurant a man and a woman sat smoking next to petite, platinum blond girls around the ages of seven and eight. The man and woman were both obese. Wiry sideburns grew along the man's jowls. The woman wore so much makeup that I could see a line along her neck and double-chin where the makeup ended according to some mysteriously-accepted cultural property line. Below this line, pale bloated flesh is acceptable; above this line, only thick foundation is allowed, made from the creamy goop siphoned out of the tanks behind fast food restaurants like this one.

It made me crazy that this was so familiar, that it felt like home. I wanted to be back in Sunnyvale, writhing around with Mandy. I wanted to kiss the clean skin on her face and throat, to crush her down and pin her lean body to the floor.

There were two ashtrays at their table, intermingled with baskets of fried okra, steak fingers, French fries and biscuits. A barn-shaped container of gravy sat dead center. The girls were wearing identical rodeo queen crowns made of paper. I took in the gravy, remembering how it tasted. Thick and salty, with flecks of pepper and traces of garlic. I could not recall the last time I'd eaten gravy on anything.

I'd been standing in the aisle for too long, staring at them. The man noticed and regarded me with wary eyes, torpid and threatening, blinking up at me through his prescription work goggles. I nodded at him and smiled, shaking off the distraction. Lurching into motion, I made my way further into the restaurant.

Someone nearby said, in disbelief, "Man...I am stuffed."

All around me, plate-glass windows looked out on the highway and nearby parking lots. The sky was filled with clouds and crisscrossed with more wires. I found a booth in the corner farthest from the smokers and sat down. Dropping my keys and wallet onto a clean spot, I checked the clock on my phone for the time. Half an hour remained; my brother Brodie wouldn't arrive for a while.

The phone vibrated just as I was about to put it down. I nearly dropped it, startled.

"Hey, guess who?"

I waited, answering when I recognized her voice. "Jenny."

She burst into excitement, giggling on the other end of the line. "I can't believe you knew it was me."

"Of course I did. How are you?"

"Good, good."

"How'd you get my number? We haven't talked in a long time."

"Yeah, I know. I got it from your step-mom. She's so sweet."

I was conflicted over this assessment of Mincy, but agreed for the sake of diplomacy. "Yes, she is...Brodie and I never would have made it without her."

"Aww."

"Though I have no idea how she lived with Dad, even for a few years."

Jenny grew more serious. "I know you're getting it from all sides, but how're you doing?"

BIG JACK is DEAD

Everything felt like a ritual. I dreaded the funeral. All the consolation, the scripted parts. "I'm okay." I tilted my head back, looking at the ceiling and blocking out the restaurant. I had the vague sense that a waitress was hovering nearby, but I ignored her. "It's not great, of course. I hadn't talked to him in a while." The sound of her breathing was audible through the phone. "What do you say when this happens? I'm not sure how I feel. I'm here, I'm seeing people..." Exasperated, I stopped in a way that caused us both to laugh.

"Well, if you've got time, I'd love to see you. I can give you a shoulder if you need one."

A thrill ran through me. "With all this...shit, that would be really nice. I miss you, Jenny."

"I miss you too." Neither of us spoke for a while then she continued, "You should come by if you get time later."

"Alright, I will. Tell me where you live."

She gave me the address, in a part of town I halfway remembered. "Behind the Presbyterian Church, right?"

She paused and said somewhat darkly, "No, we moved. We're in the trailer park now, just up the street from the church. You'll see it as you get close."

"Ah." An uncomfortable moment passed. "Well, it might help to see you."

"Great," she said. "Come by any time this evening. I ain't doing nothing."

"Alright then, it's a date."

She laughed at that. "Been a looong time since I've been on a real date, especially with you."

I chuckled, remembering the essence of our relationship in high school and just afterward. The two of us sitting through slasher movies, fondling each other in the dark, even surrounded by other people...stripping each other in her bedroom while her mother napped in the next room... skipping class, sitting in my father's truck while she went down on me...pasture parties and clumsy, drunken sex on the ground. I thought about sitting through football games together and eating at fast food places on weekend nights. The nearly constant cheating, breaking up and getting back together.

"I'll see you later," I said, "After I visit with my brother and maybe a few other people."

"Okay. Talk to you soon."

I flipped the phone shut, savoring the thought of seeing her again, the girl I'd dated for longer than anyone else.

The menu was made of cardboard, sheathed in plastic. Someone had burned a smiley face into the front cover with a cigarette. I read through the items, looking for anything remotely digestible and eventually ordering iced tea from one of the waitresses.

Brodie approached, coming down the long aisle, wearing gray pants, leather shoes with tassels, and an Oxford shirt. He was thinner than I remembered and his cheeks were hollow; I could see the bones in his face. My brother smiled and waved as he walked up. We hugged carefully.

Watching him, I felt the world shift as we sat down. I hadn't seen him for a long while. We were quiet, looking at each other, then out the window. Silence was better than mundane pleasantries. Our father's suicide was only the latest act in his long, strange influence over our lives. Through the window, I watched a family loading themselves into a four-door pickup truck.

Brodie spoke first. "Man, what do you say?" He had Dad's accent and inflection.

"Yeah, exactly. I'm not sure... What are you doing these days?"

"Selling cars again."

I cringed at the thought of being the judgmental older brother. It was too close to being the controlling father, I suppose. So I tried to be casual about my brother's decade-long addiction to painkillers. "How's the pharmaceutical situation?"

"Oh, man, I'm doing great." He gave me a blank-eyed expression that was meant to be earnest then he turned and looked out the window again. He toyed with the saltshaker, going on about "the program" and his relationship with his sponsor.

I nodded along, but I knew he was lying. When he turned back to face me, his pupils were pinpoints. They looked ridiculous, even with the light coming through the tinted glass. I let it go.

Brodie was always a tailspin for me. I kept expecting this little boy who needed my protection, who needed me to steer him clear of my father's moods. Instead I got this stranger, this car salesman; someone who borrowed drug money from everyone in the family for years before we figured out what was going on. I wanted it to be different between us, but I wasn't naïve enough to think that it could be.

"Dad would have been what this year, fifty-five?"

Brodie had always been much closer to our father and corrected me. "No, fifty-four."

After high school, I moved away from Lowfield as fast as I could. Brodie stayed behind. There were stories about Brodie fighting with our father, but mostly they got along pretty well after he got out of school.

"Was Dad seeing anyone?" I asked.

"Of course." Brodie laughed. "Always. I haven't met her, but I hear this one isn't any better than the others...the usual trash."

"Damn, Brodie." I cut my eyes at him.

He held his hands up, eyes wide. "It's true."

I turned away, looking out over the parking lot again. "Yeah." With the exception of my stepmother, my father had always been drawn to weak women. If a woman had trouble making eye contact, Dad was all over her. So my brother's description wasn't off the mark.

"You coming over to Mom's house tonight?" he asked.

I knew that he wasn't referring to our mother, but Mincy. "Yeah, for a while. I thought I'd head over after we eat."

I browsed the menu again before settling on fried catfish and a salad. Taking everything into account, these seemed safest. Another waitress in her late fifties came by and took our orders. She also refilled my tea glass and Brodie asked for a Coke just before she shuffled away.

"Something's bothering me," he said.

"Yeah?"

"I'm not sure he did it."

"Did what?" I asked, squinting at him, confused. My voice cracked when I spoke.

"Suicide." The word hung between us over the scarred tabletop.

"You don't think Dad killed himself?"

"No, I really don't." He shook his head slowly and pursed his lips. His expression was grave and concerned. He looked worried. "You might think it sounds crazy."

I reeled at the implication. It disturbed me even more that my brother could believe this, that his thinking wasn't clearer. "Brodie...Dad put a pistol in his mouth and pulled the fucking trigger. It's not like there's any doubt. He was the most fucked up person I've ever known. Mom said he used to threaten suicide to get sex on some nights. Do you know how many guns he owned? For fuck's sake, he was a walking fucking train wreck. I'm actually shocked he didn't kill himself years ago."

The old waitress was standing at our table, holding Brodie's Coke in one hand, paralyzed. I looked out the window, my face red with anger.

"Thank you," Brodie said. He gave her a car lot smile, all warmth. She set the Coke down and walked off.

"You've got to be joking," I said. "I can't believe you think that."

"Jack, I went over there. I saw that old house...the blood and everything."

BIG JACK is DEAD

I looked at my brother in disbelief. "Why the fuck would you want to do that? You didn't get enough of his shit when we were little?"

"I even went to the police station. They have photos of Dad...from the scene."

"Jesus fuck." I watched cars go by. A blackbird landed on the asphalt a few yards beyond the window and started tearing away at a carry-out container.

"You can call me nuts, but there was a cigarette on the sink. The whole thing had turned to ash, just where it was sitting. Dad never left his cigarettes like that. He always smoked them all the way down or stubbed them out." His mouth frothed a little as he spoke. "I know, because I spent a lot of my time with him."

I couldn't understand his motives, why he would believe such a thing. The crack between us crumbled and blackened with space, became a chasm, an abyss.

He went on, calmer. "I don't care what you believe. He and I sat around in that house on a bunch of different nights, talking and smoking. You haven't lived here, but I have. I knew Dad really well." He said this in a way that was prudish and superior.

I took a drink of tea to clear my mouth, which had gone dry. "That might just be the craziest fucking thing I have ever heard, little brother." I stared across at him. "So maybe Dad never let his cigarette burn all the way down...but maybe it only happened this one time because he was fucking dead." My eyes felt like they were about to pop. "I cannot believe we're even having this goddamn conversation."

"Alright," he said. His eyes were dull nickels.

"This shit isn't weird enough for you, I guess."

My brother and I sat in silence. Brodie wore a slack, disinterested look, and I slumped back into the corner of the booth. Walking by, no one would have guessed the topic of our conversation.

When the food came out, we ate it quickly without speaking. The waitress came by to refill our glasses and was surprised to find our plates empty.

"Goodness," she said, "you two eat faster than anybody I've ever seen."

"Can we get the bill?" I asked.

Her face darkened, but she rummaged through her apron and retrieved the check. "Well..." she said.

I dropped a twenty and a five on the table. "I'll get it."

Brodie gazed out across the highway, impassive. In his adult face, I could see the little kid I'd grown up with, but I was reminded once again that he was not the same person.

BIG JACK is DEAD

More than anything, I wanted to get away from him. "I'm heading over to Mom's now."

He nodded. "Okay. I'll finish this Coke and see you there."

I scooped up my keys. Outside, the humid afternoon air clung to my skin, but it felt good to leave the chilly restaurant.

Sitting in the car, I caught myself gritting my teeth. I let all the air out of my lungs. Sleep wouldn't remedy the exhaustion I felt. Glaring through the dark windshield, I focused on the blank space in front of the Lexus. My lips and mouth moved to form words that I whispered to my father. "Goddamn you."

I left the parking lot heading toward my stepmother's house, but turned toward Jenny's trailer park instead.

Chapter 9

1977

The truck rattled down the oyster shell road, kicking up puffs of white dust. In the back, a long toolbox jumped with each bump, clanking as the tools inside shifted around violently. Big Jack grunted as the truck hit a pothole, his gut bouncing in his lap. He snorted, drawing mucus into his mouth, and spat it out the window.

Jack sat on the other side of the truck, not moving save for a slight expression of disgust.

"Wanna soda?" Big Jack asked.

"Yeah," Jack said quietly.

"That sounds good, don't it?"

Jack smiled. His face was pale and unmarked. "Yeah, it does." The trace of a frown passed over his face as he spoke, a hint of shame at saying the word 'yeah' instead of 'yes, sir.' He'd been yelled at for that before, but the rule was never enforced consistently or even very often. It just came once in a while, explosively, but not often enough to make him remember it until after the fact.

Big Jack wore a thick work shirt, marked with small holes burned into place by a daily shower of welding sparks and molten slag. The shirt opened to reveal a ratty t-shirt, worn threadbare under the arms. He wore very tight Wrangler jeans and had tiny, battered cowboy boots on his unusually small feet. His face burned with shame whenever he remembered the size of his feet. He hated how small they were, thinking that this shortcoming was also tied in some way to his dick.

Big Jack wheeled the truck off the road, one-handing it into the gravel driveway of a small convenience store. The toolbox scraped across the truck bed, screeching and startling the boy as the truck jolted into the parking lot. The air outside smelled faintly of chlorine.

"Stay here," Big Jack said. "I'll be right back." He jumped down, slamming the door at his back.

Jack sat in the truck, watching through the open window, relaxing once his father was gone. A drift of dust followed the truck in from the road and settled in the hot air around the vehicle, falling like powdery rain. Jack stared, trying to trace individual particles as they floated downward. He could taste the dust on the air inside the cab of the truck, which otherwise smelled like oil and tools. Using one of his small hands, he lifted the collar of his shirt to cover his mouth and nose. He breathed through the cloth, filtering out the dust and fantasizing about being a desperado, getting ready to rob a train.

On the horizon just over the low treeline, boiler stacks from one of the nearby petrochemical plants rose like a pair of corroded gray flutes, embedded in the ground. The identical stacks stood high in the air, skeletal ladders running up the sides, leading to small catwalks near the top. A twelve foot flame rose up from one of them as the plant burned off excess gas byproduct. The plant was known as *Bardiché* by everyone within fifty miles. Jack studied the flame.

Another battered truck pulled up, grinding and slinging gravel, and another cloud of fine dust rolled in and began to settle. The truck came to a stop in front of the convenience store and a hefty man opened the door. He slid his ass off the seat and stepped out, dressed like Jack's father in jeans and thick, flame-retardant shirt. The jeans were tucked into his leather boots, which passed for rakish among the plant workers. His belly was distended far forward, like something grafted onto his frame. He wore a pair of prescription work glasses with dark plastic guards attached to the sides. The handle of the knife hanging from his belt had been wrapped and re-wrapped with layers of duct tape.

BIG JACK is DEAD

Slipping further down in the truck, Jack struggled to contain a laugh. He imagined himself screaming the word pig out the window. The notion came to him without provocation. He held his collar up over his mouth again and watched the man over the edge of the dashboard.

The man coughed and tried to suck in some of his gut before entering the store. He emerged a few minutes later eating a Butterfinger bar. His unshaven face was partially covered by his own hammy fist and the candy bar wrapper as he passed the open truck window. His eyes carried the weight of his sullenness while his mouth worked the Butterfinger bar. As he passed, he locked eyes with Jack, but the boy kept his expression blank. A few feet on, the man opened the door to his truck, put one booted foot up into place and grabbed the steering wheel, hauling himself up into the seat. He bucked his hips, shifting over onto the seat of the truck, which groaned like bed springs. Taking in an enormous wad of candy bar, he started the truck and backed out, creating another wave of dust.

Half an hour later, Big Jack came out of the convenience store carrying a Shasta. He climbed into the truck, got situated and handed the drink to his son. It was half-empty and warm, but Jack was happy to have it. He took a sip, feeling the carbonation, the sugar, and the acid hit his mouth all at once. Everything else in the world went away and he leaned his head back, taking a long, burning pull from the aluminum can.

Big Jack sat behind the wheel, watching the boy drink. "Goddamn, son. You are such a fucking glutton." His chin was directly over his right shoulder, jowls quivering and face flush. He raised his right fist to hit the boy, but the cramped interior of the truck restricted his movement. Unable to swing, he grew flustered and lowered his hand.

Jack held the Shasta can sheepishly. The contempt in his father's voice stunned him even without a physical blow. He felt the calluses on Big Jack's hand as he reached over and took the drink.

Still seething, Big Jack killed the Shasta in a couple of swigs. Then he started up the engine and crushed the gas pedal with one of his small boots. The truck kicked up a spray of white gravel and raced away like an out of control sled.

Chapter 10

1999

The drive from the restaurant only took five minutes. I parked under a pecan tree, where a pair of squirrels chased each other up the trunk and through the branches, making muscled leaps from one limb to another. Searching around, it took a minute to find the right number. Jenny's trailer was one of roughly two dozen units. Walking toward it, I crushed a pecan against the asphalt. Unlike some of the trailers, there were no toys out front, no Christmas lights around the windows, no potted plants on the porch. I stood on the thin metal steps and knocked. The door made a strange rattling sound, thin layers of fiberglass and aluminum.

Jenny opened up. "Look at you, stranger." She beamed, her eyes flitting over my face, following the faint scar running up through my eyebrow. I smiled back, but flinched internally; two of her teeth were now gold.

"Come in. My husband's in Baton Rouge, on-site for the company, so we got the place to ourselves."

The interior of the trailer was dark. The air conditioner shook the walls and I could feel a breeze blowing up from a floor vent set in the carpet. I looked at Jenny and tried to remember her as a teenager. Her skin was weathered now, but she still wore thick blue eye shadow. She was lean and wiry, a few inches shorter than me. Unlike most of the women on the Gulf Coast, she had not blown up like a trophy-winning sow. Genetics, I suppose. Wrapping her up in a slow hug, I whispered over her shoulder, "Been a long time."

"It's good to see you too."

And it was. We hugged for a while, rocking in place. I pressed my mouth against the skin at the base of her neck, where it met her collarbone. She didn't say anything.

"Sorry I'm only down here because of the funeral."

Softening as she remembered the reason for my visit, she said, "Yeah, I'm so sorry about your daddy. He was a good man."

I thought about biting her, *tearing into the soft skin on her shoulder*. It just flashed through my head. I held back an angry response and kissed the side of her throat. "Thank you for saying that and for having me over." I backed away and smiled, trying to lift my mood.

She leaned back, letting me hold her weight against falling, her eyes locked on mine. "I catch myself thinking about you a lot," she said. "You don't come home that often."

"You're the only thing I miss."

She laughed. "You live so far away, out there in California. I've thought about taking a drive, coming to see you."

"You could. It's really nice."

"That would be so much fun, to get away from here for a while." She hesitated. "It almost killed me when you moved."

"I know. I felt bad." We stared at each other while I thought about the ways in which we had been intertwined. As if we were dancing, I put my hands on her hips and pulled her closer. She settled into my arms and we swayed in place, making her laugh against my ear. "What would have happened between us if I had stayed?"

She creased her brow, but didn't speak.

"Sorry," I said. "I couldn't stay here, with my dad."

Looking down, she nodded.

Taking a step, I moved us over to the sofa. I sat, dragging her down with me, encircling her with one arm and pulling her near. She settled in, draping one of her legs over my lap.

"Maybe I should have gone somewhere too," she said in a quiet voice. "Off and on, I think about those days, especially when things aren't going so well."

We passed time in silence, just enjoying the proximity.

"After all this shit with dad, it's good to see a friendly face."

"Good. Glad I can help."

"I don't even feel sad. It's just weird."

She looked concerned, studying me.

"Dad, my family...I try not to think about them. Even lunch with my brother today was difficult."

"I'm sorry," she said. "You both went through a lot. I thought you got along with him."

I frowned, not sure what to say. "He's different. Hard to describe." A phrase came into mind, *California is my religion.*

She leaned her head against me. Reaching up, I brushed my fingers through one of her curls, tracing the skin of her neck. "Tell me about what you're doing."

She let her head fall back against the sofa. "There's not much to tell. I've been living with Leonard and he's been working different jobs with the company. The pay is good when he gets enough overtime." She started to say something else, but trailed off.

Her thigh was warm against my belly and lap. I toyed with her hair. "Wish I could blow off the funeral and stay here."

She laughed softly. "That'd just make it worse for everyone else."

"Yeah, maybe."

"No, it would," she said. "They need to see you."

I looked away from her for a second, actually thinking about my father suddenly, thinking about the last time I'd seen him. After a minute, I found her eyes, tilting my head and leaning closer. "I really want to kiss you."

When Jenny spoke, her voice was low, her forehead wrinkled in determination. "Then kiss me."

I leaned into her, inhaling perfume and traces of cigarette smoke, feeling her small breasts flatten against me. The texture of her skin and the smell of her hair were familiar. Our faces came together. I cupped her breasts and she moaned into my mouth. Our hands roamed over each other like they had a decade before. She began rubbing me through my pants. Mid-kiss, she tried to unbuckle my pants, fumbling blindly with the zipper. I pushed her hand aside, jerked the belt open and tore the flap down. She stuck her tongue deeper into my mouth then dropped her head into my lap. As her lips wrapped around me, I collapsed back against the couch, raising my hips in time with her movements. I cried out when I came, warmth flooding through me and my mind going blank, the obliteration of release.

Sitting there with my eyes closed, I remembered a night from just after high school. I drove her out under a lonely bridge, stopping at a spot where people went crabbing during the day. The bridge was located in the middle of a stretch of county highway separating Lowfield and Quailbury. Cow pastures flanked the road on either side and the moon was bright. Talking on the phone an hour or two before, I convinced her to lie to her fiancé, to meet with me.

She sat up in the semi-darkness of the trailer. She leaned against me, my pants still down around my thighs. We alternated between talking and nuzzling before moving to the bedroom. Propped up on all the pillows in her bed, I asked about her husband.

Weasel-like, her face drew into a snarl. "He's a fat asshole. I hate him."

I was genuinely surprised by her intensity. "That's fucking terrible."

"Yeah." She exhaled a deep sigh. Smiling sheepishly, she dropped her voice. "I've been seeing someone else. He's a foreman over in Plant B and has his own boat." She covered her face in excitement and I laughed. *Which one of these guys are we actually cheating on?*

We made love without a condom and drank cold, bottled beer in bed.

"Tomorrow is the funeral," she said.

"Yes it is." I took a long pull, bringing the bottle to rest on my belly, relishing the sweating glass. I studied her, nestled beside me. "I'm glad I got to see you."

She smiled at me. "Yeah." She looked away, at the curtained window. The dying sun lit up the yellow cloth, turning it to white gold. "You never would have been happy here."

I raised my eyebrows. "No argument there," I said. It was still hard to connect with anyone. Nothing was exactly right; it always felt like something bad was about to happen.

"We'd have just ended up cheating on each other anyway," I said.

She laughed and slapped my chest playfully. "I wouldn't have...maybe you, mister." A beat later, she gestured vaguely across the bedroom with her beer. "Okay, you're right."

We laughed and she put her head against my shoulder. All along my body, I could feel our skin touching, hot in some places, cool in others.

"I hope you're coming tomorrow. It would help."
"I will," she said. "Don't worry."
We got dressed and I drove back to the motel.

Chapter 11

1979

Jack walked beneath a sky the color of crumbling Christmas tinsel. A line of black clouds lay across the horizon and the wind pushed at his back, occasionally lifting the hood on his windbreaker. His backpack was slung over one shoulder, full of middle school texts and a rusted lunch box. He made his way past a large vacant lot where chain-link backstops capped two corners of the field parenthetically and a weed-covered levee ran along the far side. A small utility building stood on a concrete slab near one of the backstops.

With furtive glances, Jack watched a skinny girl walking on the opposite sidewalk across the street. Roughly his age, her name was Jenny. She wore bell-bottom jeans and a sweatshirt covered in hearts. He saw her almost every day because they had science class together, but they rarely spoke. She was reserved; tentative in a way that was appealing to him.

When he reached his block he ran for a while just to feel his legs move. Hoisting the backpack higher, he took off down the sidewalk, concentrating on moving fast but keeping his sneakers as quiet as possible. One of his favorite books told the story of a heroic field mouse who wielded a needle, using it like a sword against a clan of predatory rooks. Sprinting along, Jack fantasized about a huge blackbird chasing him. High above, the bird tilted its head, regarding him with shiny eyes. He stopped running after half a block, breathing deeply for a few more paces and finally blowing out a huge breath before settling into a walk.

Big Jack's truck was in the driveway and the garage door was open. Inside, his father was messing around at his tool bench.

Jack stopped just between the truck and the doorway. Studying his father, he let his backpack sag to the concrete, dangling it from a shoulder strap. "Hi, Dad."

"Hey, boy."

Jack watched his father shuffle things around, hanging a set of wrenches on a pegboard rack. He really had nothing to say to his father and Big Jack rarely spoke except when he wanted something or was angry. Jack felt uncomfortable in the silence. He tried to think of something to say, but couldn't. Leaving seemed wrong somehow. Walking away without speaking would draw his father's ire.

Big Jack picked up a wrench and tested its weight in his hand. He fished a roll of pipefitter's tape out of his jeans and tossed it onto the workbench. He seemed perplexed by the collection of objects in front of him. The workbench itself was so saturated with grease that the wood was black and the garage perpetually smelled like the insides of an engine. Jack smelled the odor every time he walked through the kitchen past the door leading into the garage.

"What'd you do at the school today?" Big Jack asked, still looking down at the tools strewn out along the bench.

Jack swallowed to counter the dead feeling in his throat. "Nothing," he said quietly.

"Nothing?" Big Jack turned to look at his son a few feet away. His wiry hair stood out from his head in tufts, molded and mussed all day by his welding cap. "You didn't do no school work? You didn't run no laps in gym? You didn't talk to nobody?" Big Jack's eyes were a little too wide, bulging slightly with challenge. His voice carried a sarcastic undertone.

Jack stared at his father, aware of the truck parked behind him. A strange heat was coming off the engine and the boy could feel it. He could smell the dead insects embedded in the front grill of the vehicle. "Yes, sir," he said, "I did school work. And I talked to people."

"During class?" asked Big Jack.

"No, sir. I listened in class."

Big Jack tried to detect some sign of falsehood. "Yeah, I bet you did." His interest waned and he turned back to the tools in front of him. Scratching one side of his face absently, he left a grease streak there. The vein in the center of his forehead stood out freakishly, as it always did when he was puzzled or angry, which was almost a constant.

The kitchen door jangled and swung out. Brodie stood on the step, just inside the house. There was a guilty expression stretched over his face. Jack and his father turned to regard the young boy. Jack felt afraid for his brother.

Brodie looked down at the concrete floor of the garage. "There's something wrong with Boss Hog," he said.

Boss Hog was Brodie's hamster. The tan, chubby rodent lived in a cage in the boys' bedroom.

"Go see," Big Jack said. He reached into a small tin of washers and fished around for one of a particular size.

Jack was happy to have a way out of the encounter with his father, but concerned about his brother. He crossed the garage and entered the kitchen, leaning his backpack against the dishwasher. Brodie stepped aside and followed sheepishly.

In the living room, down among some of Brodie's toys, Boss Hog was in a bad way, dragging himself along through the carpet. Jack walked over and sank to the floor. The hamster was making steady progress toward some unknown destination, but his back legs trailed behind him uselessly. Jack made an unconscious sound as he watched the small thing. A dull sensation swam through his chest, paralyzing him as it spread to the rest of his body, a leaden fatigue that caused his arms to droop.

"What happened, Brodie?"

The younger boy spoke quietly. "He bit me and I slinged him into that wall." He started crying.

"It's okay. Let me see." He reached over and took Brodie's hand, prying it open. "You're all right...it barely left a mark."

Boss Hog still crawled along on his front legs, advancing a few more inches.

"You go to your room and I'll take Boss Hog to Dad. Okay?"

Brodie stopped crying. He nodded and walked off, skirting his wounded hamster and pausing to scoop up a superhero action figure.

When his brother was gone, Jack got lower to the floor and inspected Boss Hog more closely. Tears welled up in his eyes as the hamster pulled itself through the dense carpet. Jack stroked it once, very gently, from the top of its head to the base of its stubby tail. Boss Hog ducked, but otherwise

116

didn't react, continuing his slow passage toward the den, according to his own arcane compass.

Hearing the door to the garage open, Jack called out to the kitchen, "Dad? Can you come help?"

"What is it?" Big Jack came into the room holding a monkey wrench.

"Boss Hog bit Brodie," Jack reported. "I think Brodie dropped him and now he can't walk."

Big Jack came closer, taking stock of the situation. He towered over the hamster, but was only slightly taller than his twelve year old son. Grunting, Big Jack knelt. He made a quick diagnosis after watching the hamster. "Back's broke."

Jack let out a soft breath. He knew from TV that nothing survived a broken back.

"Here," Big Jack said. "Let's take him into the kitchen." With a meaty, but careful gesture, he herded Boss Hog into his hand. He straightened and walked into the kitchen, holding the hamster in one hand and the monkey wrench in the other.

Jack followed his father quietly, pride competing with sadness; he was doing something with his father that Brodie was too young to do.

In the kitchen, Big Jack set Boss Hog onto a dishtowel. "Don't let him get away."

BIG JACK is DEAD

Jack stood at the counter, looking down at the hamster while cradling it in the dishtowel. He eased it back onto the towel each time it tried to crawl. He felt like a soldier with a minor, but important role to play.

Big Jack set the wrench down and moved over to the walk-in pantry. Digging around in the dark, he came back with one of the plastic baggies his wife used to wrap up his sandwiches for lunch. At the stove, he turned on the back burner, which no one ever used because the pilot light was broken. He sidestepped a little to get closer to Boss Hog and Jack moved out of the way.

Big Jack picked up the hamster and gingerly eased it into the plastic baggie. He stole a glance at his son next to him at the counter. "This way, he won't feel nothing. The gas'll just put him to sleep."

Jack nodded. A cold calm come over him. The small animal was injured beyond repair and this was the only way. He accepted his father's judgment without question. The boy mouthed the words, "Goodbye" as the smell of gas filled the kitchen. The broken back burner, the one his mother had cursed many times, hissed out the invisible air that would put Boss Hog to sleep forever.

Big Jack moved a step closer to the stove with the baggie. Inside, Boss Hog pushed against the plastic cocoon with his front legs, testing it and wiggling his whiskered nose. Big Jack held the baggy up to the burner, off to the side, trapping as much of the gas as he could.

Jack moved so he could get a better view of the scene, face solemn as he watched.

Somehow the broken pilot light ignited, creating a burst of flame like a magic trick. It happened so fast that both Jack and his father were stunned. The small bag melted around Boss Hog in a split second, burning up his whiskers and coating him with molten plastic and fire. The hamster emitted a horrible scree sound, struggling spastically as Big Jack flung the entire mess down onto the stove.

"Goddammit," he said. His face constricted in disbelief as he shouldered his son aside and snatched up the monkey wrench. Big Jack brought the wrench down so fast on the flaming, struggling creature that the wrench dented the sheet-metal surface of the stove. The fire around Boss Hog was snuffed out by the blow and his skull was crushed in the same instant.

Lips drawn back, Jack looked down at the smoking remains. The hamster's body was covered in a blackened sheath. Its forelegs stretched up plaintively toward the ceiling. Jack could make out one of the tiny, articulated hands where it emerged from the melted baggie. The claws were somehow pristine, tiny points of translucent nail splayed out fiercely. A last streamer of smoke wisped upward before fading from sight. The kitchen smelled of burnt plastic.

Big Jack dropped the wrench on the counter and ran his hand over his forehead. "Goddammit, I didn't mean for that to happen. Goddammit." He looked at the burner in wild shock. It held a perfect crown of flame. Big Jack looked at his son. "That thing don't never light…it just don't. It ain't never worked."

Jack stood stunned and mute.

Big Jack used the dishtowel to scoop up the remains of the hamster. He took three quick steps to the pantry and threw the entire bundle, towel and all, into the trash.

There was a papery rustle from the entrance of the narrow kitchen. Both Jack and his father turned to the doorway, where Brodie stood leaning back against the refrigerator. Colored magnets fell to the floor behind him and one of his elementary school drawings floated after them. He called out, wailing, "*Daddy, why did you do that to Boss Hog?*"

Jack crept back into the kitchen later that evening. The dinner dishes sat heaped in the sink. In the den, Jack's father and mother watched television with the lights out. The volume was up loud and light flickered at the edge of the dark kitchen. Walking quietly in his socked feet, Jack stole over to the pantry.

He tried to find Boss Hog's body in the dark, but could not. The smell of coffee, rotting vegetables and roach killer rose up from the trash. Holding his breath, he eased the pantry door closed at his back, stepping down six inches onto the concrete floor. A knotted cord hung overhead. When he tugged it, dim light lit the pantry.

Rooting around, he shoveled aside a pile of cold macaroni and cheese, finally locating the hamster's remains. It sickened him throughout dinner, knowing that Boss Hog was down in the trash a few feet from the table, wrapped in the dishtowel.

Jack lifted the bundle out and brushed coffee grounds from the towel. Reaching up again, he turned out the pantry light with his left hand. In the darkness, he pushed the door open and moved to the far end of the kitchen. The back door let him into the yard and he breathed again only when he was away, out in the night air.

On the side of the house, he moved to the edge of the porch light. Crickets chirped in every direction. He set Boss Hog's rag-wrapped body on the ground and looked around in search of his mother's trowel. Ramona almost never used it and the yard was in dismal shape. However, every few months she got the urge to go into the backyard and dig around, entertaining visions of some grand landscaping scheme that she usually abandoned within the hour. Jack found the rusty trowel sitting on a small wall made of cinder blocks, originally intended to contain a tomato garden. He brought it back to the base of the tree where the grisly package waited. He knelt and started digging. After the hole was eight inches deep, he paused and looked down at the dark earth. His own body blocked most of the light, making it hard to see. There was enough light to make out the dishtowel, the hole and the glinting trowel.

Tears formed in his eyes. He had rarely played with Boss Hog, but he could see the hamster running on its wheel, feet a blur. The cage smelled of urine because Jack hardly ever changed the wood shavings. He choked out high-pitched sobs and his cheeks ran with hot streaks.

The dishtowel was damp under his hand as he arranged it tighter around the body. The melted bag had hardened and he could barely feel Boss Hog at all through the plastic and the towel. The bundle crackled in his hands. Reverently, he placed it into the hole then set a nearby brick down into the grave with equal care, covering the hamster's body to protect it from dogs, opossums or anything else digging around in the yard. Filling the hole with dirt, he used the trowel to cover the brick entirely, patting the earth smooth as he put Boss Hog to rest.

As Jack turned away from the tree, a wood roach launched itself from one of the branches not far away, gliding past. It flew upright as it *whirred* by and landed with a tap against the siding close to the kitchen window. Jack cringed, looking at the thing, a dark spot on the wall. Even the sound of its flight filled him with loathing.

Skirting wide and moving with stealth, he made his way to the back door and went inside, hands covered in dirt.

Chapter 12

1999

Standing at the mirror, dressing for my father's funeral, I found myself wondering how many people had fucked in my motel room. A slide show of couples went through my mind, holding each other down, thrusting against one another with anger, betraying someone else, crying out with sounds that could have been anguish or ecstasy. I worked on my tie, pulling it too tight against my throat, then leaned close to the reflection as my fingers loosened the knot.

The funeral was scheduled to start at four, but there was a casket viewing for family and friends earlier in the day. I planned on attending both, but wasn't sure why. When I was young, I treated my father like some sort of wild animal, approaching him with caution or avoiding him altogether. Later, he just seemed tired and pathetic...broken. He brought me into the world then used me as a dumping ground for hate until the day I was strong enough to wage war in return. That defined our relationship, so why bother?

Long before his death, I worked as a temporary employee at a Web-based start-up. I'd just moved to California and the job consisted of testing the company's software and entering bugs into a database. Explaining it to Dad was difficult; he barely grasped the concept of working on something—manufacturing something—that did not exist in the physical world.

Confusion ran across his face, eyes cut to the side, watching me warily as we sat together at his wobbly dinner table. It was early in the morning. Dad was smoking and drinking coffee. I told him that I was only making eight dollars an hour and that I sat in the back of a warehouse at a folding table.

Recognition dawned in his eyes. He nodded vigorously and seemed to recognize the type of work I was doing. For a second, I thought there might be some kind of connection between us, over work if nothing else. Then he said, "That's a woman's job, boy. You'll get something better later on."

I studied him, deflated.

He asked, "Hey, they got plants out there, don't they?"

I took over the quality assurance department by the age of twenty-eight, doubling my father's blue collar wages. After that I moved into an amorphous production role that took advantage of my personality and strengths. By then my salary quadrupled Dad's pay. I called him each time I got another bump, chatting with him before mentioning that I had good news. He was always excited at first, seeing any increase in pay as a blow struck against the bosses. But when I told him how much money I was making, he stopped smoking for a while as he fought with my words.

"That can't be right, can it? They really givin' you that much?" Silence passed and I could hear the bones in his back snapping and popping. This was almost supernaturally satisfying, this silence coming through the other end of the line.

Maybe death was the final mastery. He was gone. Buzzards wheeled high over his spirit, a black mobile over a crib. The funeral signaled the last stage of the long ritual between the two of us.

I was finished with the knot of my tie, but I stood in front of the mirror, arms down at my sides, thinking about how he'd lived his entire life on the Gulf Coast. Over thirty years working in the chemical plants scattered across the same county where he was born. Thirty years walking through that concrete and salt grass landscape, under rusted skies made of pipes and catwalks...in a shower of molten slag, breathing the chlorinated air that hugged the ground for miles.

He married and divorced six times and that didn't even touch upon the countless women he met in the white trash dive bars, redneck diners and trailer parks dotting the region. His attraction to women like my mother, wounded in spirit, was a kind of magnetic force that he could never escape.

His life must have been an endless series of shocking disappointments. His mother's coldness and his father's violence, a string of broken relationships, decades of meaningless toil in a toxic atmosphere. How many times had I dashed his dreams? He wanted a son who played quarterback or brought home a trophy deer every year. I started to laugh, but the laughter died on my face.

Dad had lived a life of pain and failure that lasted over half a century. Once the final decision was made, once his finger was irrevocably committed to the act of pulling the trigger (*squeezing slowly, breath held, to keep the gun from kicking*), it must have been the sweetest release he'd ever known. I felt sorry for him and no emotion could have stunned me more. Under that, there was something else, a longing for some version of my father that never existed.

Pulling out my phone, I dialed the short number.

The operator responded, "Nine-one-one...what's the nature of your emergency."

"Can you transfer me to the police station? I need the non-emergency line."

"Hold please." The line went quiet.

BIG JACK is DEAD

A woman answered after a second, stating her name and saying something else so quickly from habit that I couldn't follow.

"Hello. This is delicate, but I need your help with something."

"Okay, sir, go ahead."

"My father killed himself a couple of days ago..." I gave her time to grasp the words.

"I'm very sorry to hear that. What can I do for you?"

"I need to talk to the officer who was in charge of the investigation, I suppose." I never dealt with law enforcement and had no idea whether anyone had been in charge or whether there had even been an investigation. "I have some questions about...how they found my father."

"I understand. I'm so sorry, dear. Hold for a moment." A pre-recorded public service announcement began to play over the phone, warning me of the fines and penalties associated with driving while intoxicated.

Someone else picked up the line. "This is Officer Ramirez. Can I help you?"

"Hello, yes, my name is Jack Hickman. Junior. My father's name was also Jack Hickman. He killed himself a couple of days ago and I'm here trying to get everything taken care of. The funeral, his things and my family. I just wanted to ask you about some of this."

"You're the oldest son," Ramirez said.

"Right."

"I met with your little brother, Brodie."

"Yeah, he mentioned it." I looked down at the floor, thinking about what my brother had done. "I was just wondering what you could tell me over the phone."

"Well, Jack Hickman committed suicide, as you said. With a handgun, two days ago." Unlike the woman who had been on the phone earlier, Ramirez's voice contained no trace of empathy. "I have the address if you need it."

I pressed my lips together. "No, that's not necessary. I just...I wanted to know something." It was hard to ask. "Was there a note?"

"No." Ramirez said the word flatly. "There was nothing like that at the scene of the investigation."

I rolled my eyes to the ceiling, seeing images of my father's final home in snapshot form, taken from the crazy, tilted angles of murder scene photos on TV. Except that no one murdered my father; he did it himself. I saw his body on the floor of the old rental house, legs twisted beneath him, face hidden. His t-shirt was soaked with blood and his scarred cowboy boots jutted up in the foreground. The lighting was harsh, reflecting off against my father's skin, making it shockingly white. Shadows crept in from the corners of the room.

I wondered what this man Ramirez knew. Had he drawn an outline in chalk? Had he recorded the precise angle of the body and the location of all the bits of flesh that must have been scattered through the room, matted pieces of hair or brain. Did he make jokes? *Know what the last thing that went through his mind was?*

My legs felt unstable beneath me and my voice was raspy. "It's just, I've heard…" Thoughts came into my head like half-blind birds crippled by impact with a window. "I've heard that most of the time, in the overwhelming number of suicides, there's a note. They almost always leave a note."

"No, sir. There was no note. We looked."

I waited for the world to become solid again. Drifting over to the bathroom, I leaned against the doorjamb. "Are you sure?" My voice was quiet, but I had already given up. I knew the answer.

"Yes, I am. We went over the house like we always do, according to our procedures. We conducted an investigation and looked at everything. His belongings were transferred to a storage facility at the request of the nearest local relative…a former wife, I believe."

I took several breaths, studying myself in the mirror. My eyes were hollows looking back. I reached up and touched my face.

"Is there anything else you can tell me?"

Officer Ramirez weighed his words. "Your daddy knew what he was doing."

I closed my eyes again. "Okay. I...appreciate your time."

"Not a problem. I regret what you've had to go through. That's all I can tell you over the phone. If you need anything more, you can stop by the station. Now, Mr. Hickman, is that all?"

"Yes." What else was there? He waited quietly for me to hang up.

Brodie stood on the steps behind the funeral home, smoking a cigarette. I waved at him as I wheeled the car around. He waved back, holding the cigarette up, but his expression was dead.

As I got out of the car, he called out to me across the parking lot. "What happened?"

"Sorry I didn't make it."

"Where'd you go after you left? Mom freaked out. You wouldn't answer your phone. A bunch of people showed up at her place."

"I didn't feel like socializing," I said. Leaning on a metal railing, I stayed far enough away to avoid his smoke.

One side of his mouth lifted and his brows came together. "That's it?"

"Yeah...I didn't feel like answering questions and all that. So I sat in my motel room. I felt like shit."

"Damn." He took a drag and looked away.

"Sorry if that threw people for a loop, but I wouldn't have been good company anyway." I watched him as I spoke, trying to see my little brother inside this man. When I made eye contact, he looked away. There were lines at the corners of his eyes that made him look weak. He had Dad's eyes.

Brodie looked me over. "You look really good at least."

"Thanks."

The back door to the funeral home flew open and Mincy came out onto the steps. Short and heavy even when Brodie and I were young, my stepmother had gained weight, adding to her hen-like appearance. Most of her weight, for whatever reason, was in her ass and in the backside of her thighs. Her legs were like pillars of white clay and her ass was like a beanbag chair that someone had glued to her backside. She had hair that curled up in back like a duck's tail.

"Jack! Where in God's name were you? I had a house full of people last night." Her tone implied some catastrophic occurrence.

My throat tightened and I glared at her. "Jesus, Mom, calm down." Five seconds and she was digging into me already. "I was at the El Cinco. I felt way too bad to go out."

"Well, my God. We were expecting you. We had food and guests." Her eyes rolled up so that I could see the whites. She stepped closer and I had to tilt my head down to look at her. "You could have called," she said.

"Well, I didn't call. I told you, I felt bad. I didn't want to go out. I didn't want to see anyone."

She looked up at me, her mouth making an ugly line. Her voice dropped lower and her hands balled into fists. "You only ever think of yourself, don't you? You've always been like that...you don't care about anyone else."

"Do you have to say shit like that?"

Brodie watched us impassively, flat again.

"Well, what was I supposed to think? You worried me sick last night. Do you know the first thing that came into my mind? Do you?" Her voice was shrill and her eyes rolled upward again.

"No. What the fuck came into your mind?" I braced myself, held my breath.

She leaned in closer. "I was worried that you'd followed in your father's footsteps."

"Oh, goddammit. Get off me!" I shouted and the words echoed across the funeral home parking lot. Rising up from the weeds in the field beyond, blackbirds raced toward the roof.

Mincy went silent. Her eyes widened and the muscles in her face tightened. Her dark head was shot with gray straggles, resisting the hairspray. The space behind the funeral home was so quiet that I heard the wet pucker as Brodie put the cigarette to his lips and sucked on it.

"Alright, Jack," she said. "Next time please just call."

Childhood memories clawed their way up. I remembered all the times she told me I didn't care about anyone else, remembering how she pushed my Dad to dump my mother. "Sure. Next time Dad kills himself, I'll try to be more considerate. I'll try to think about your goddamn dinner plans."

She started to speak, but stopped, shoulders falling. "I just want to make things right, Jack." The fight had left her. "We're not a family any more, but I just want to make things right."

HARVEY SMITH

When Brodie exhaled a lungful of smoke, I turned toward him. "That is fucking nasty. How do you smoke that shit after watching them do it for so many years?"

He met my eyes, shrugging and taking another drag.

"There are much faster ways to fuck yourself up," I said. Going inside, I left them both standing on the steps.

Within the cool air of the funeral home, some of my anger slipped away. I stopped and leaned against a wall next to a pastoral watercolor. A herd of deer stood near a lake. I breathed deep a few times, hating the way I fought with my family; trying to forget them. This place was soothing. Dim lighting and faint music. It was a calculated effect, but it helped.

The main hall was wide and connected all the rooms dedicated to viewings and services. An ornate rug ran the length of the hall and ceramic urns stood every ten feet. Most of the doors off the main hall were closed, covered over by heavy curtains. There was only one open room. The doors were propped back and the curtains were drawn wide, held by braided ropes. I followed the prerecorded organ music, which grew louder as I approached. Under the arched doorway, I found myself twenty feet from my father's coffin.

BIG JACK is DEAD

Past several cushioned chairs, the casket sat under a strip of track lights. Visible through the opening in the casket, my father's face was lit up. As the seconds passed, I had no awareness of time. My mind struggled to take in the image before me. No one else was around. I licked my lips and took a few steps into the room. There were no rules for this moment that made sense. I half expected a queue of people, standing in line, or for someone to ask me for a ticket. Music continued to play from hidden speakers as I approached and looked down into the coffin.

Though he was thin, Dad looked perfect, as if resting. There were deep grooves around his eyes, but his face was relaxed. He looked younger because someone had shaved him. This defined his lips, making them look more delicate. He wore a plain suit and his hands were folded atop his chest as if guarding his heart. There was no sign of a gunshot wound on his head, no trace of powder burns on his mouth.

Without thinking about it, I touched his skin, cupping his folded hands under my palm. They were cool and dry, inhumanly solid, like they were made of hardened wax. I rested my hand there, staring at his face. I felt like I was underwater. His time in the world had ended. Seeing him in that way, unable to affect anything ever again, a strange sense of tension slipped away from me.

My eyes got misty, but some reflex closed that down. Lifting my hand away, I continued to stare, fascinated. Unable to help it, I wiped my hand on my pants leg.

The music went quiet, pausing between songs. Sitting down on one of the couches, I leaned forward and steepled my fingers in front of me. Dad's coffin sat in the center of the room, but I was confused as to what I was supposed to feel. I just felt dead.

Chapter 13

1979

Jack was lying on the couch with a comic book. He'd stopped reading and was staring into the air. He imagined himself among the outcasts from the comic, living in a Victorian estate near London. Tears welled up in his eyes as he saw himself sitting next to a fireplace with his caring mentor. Later, he walked along the edge of a pond with one of the superhero girls who lived at the estate. They held hands and leaned close in the evening air. They sat on a bench and kissed. Jack stiffened in his shorts as he thought about her becoming a cat in the middle hours of the night, sneaking into his bedroom and returning to girl form, standing bare in the center of the room, climbing into his bed.

An engine roared down the street and he lifted his head from the couch cushion. Outside, his father's truck banked hard and bounced into the driveway, groaning springs and sliding rubber. The headlights came through the blinds, lighting up the living room, stretching across the wall and onto the ceiling. Jack sat up as the truck door creaked and slammed. His face burned and he sat paralyzed, wondering what he was supposed to be doing.

Big Jack walked through the door carrying his battered lunch box. It looked too large for his body, swinging around from a busted handle. Nearly everyone who worked at the plant carried a similar contraption. Ramona packed it each morning at 5AM, filling it with the same fare every day: a coffee thermos, two sandwiches, a bag of potato chips, a dill pickle and a stack of chocolate chip cookies, wrapped in a paper towel. Big Jack struggled to un-tuck his scorched shirt, finally loosening his belt buckle, which was half-covered by his gut. The belt was etched with mustang horses, stained to look like a brand. Jack remembered the way the horses felt against his face.

"Goddamn shutdown's over," Big Jack said. "Worked overtime for four weeks straight. Fuckin' time-and-a-half pay." From the center of the living room, he looked at his son sitting on the couch. "Whatcha doin', boy?"

"Reading," Jack said, holding up the comic. He felt disrespectful sitting down while talking to his father, so he stood up.

"Funny books?"

"Yeah."

"Ain't you a little old for that?" Big Jack stood with his arms down at his sides, clutching the lunch box in one gnarled hand. His face carried a trace of repulsion. "Ain't you ten?"

"Twelve." Jack could smell his father now, a familiar mélange of industrial odors...metal shavings and chlorine. Big Jack smelled like the underbelly of a train. Jack sensed that his father was in a good mood. He smiled. "I like the fights."

"Ha!" Big Jack said. "Batman's an ass-beater." Big Jack laughed then dropped his voice. "Man, I'd sure like to fuck that girl who plays Catlady on TV." He gazed into space and Jack looked down at the floor.

"Boy, you excited?"

Jack's mind reeled as he remembered something that, until that second, he'd forgotten. His stomach lurched. Deer season started tomorrow, which meant that he and his father were leaving for four days. He made himself smile. "Yeah... it's gonna be great, I bet."

"Damn, straight," Big Jack said. "I'm gonna kill a buck!" With a lighter step, he walked into the kitchen. Jack heard the lunch box slam onto the counter and slide through some mail or other papers scattered about. Big Jack bellowed, throwing his voice off every wall in the house, "Hey, Ramona! Where are them goddamn huntin' tags?"

Jack stared at the living room wall. Thinking about spending several days on the deer lease, he sighed. Shuffling off to his bedroom, he carried the comic neatly at his side, careful not to bend it. He had hunted with his father the year before, though back then he was too young to actually hunt. This year he was taking his father's old rifle and would get his own deer stand. This year he was expected to kill something.

Jack dreaded spending time alone with his father. It would take five hours on the highways of East Texas just to reach the property. The two of them would stay together in a shack, returning Monday. Ramona and Brodie were staying behind.

Jack contemplated feigning sickness, but discarded the idea because it might seem too sudden. He lay in bed, looking out the window. There were no curtains and he could see the night sky just over the neighbor's roof.

Big Jack stepped into the room. "You packed for tomorrow?"

"No, sir," Jack said.

"Well, goddamn, boy." He looked alarmed, horrified. "What the fuck you waitin' for? We got to leave at five in the goddamn morning. Get a move on."

Jack rolled up out of the bed and pulled open the chest of drawers in the corner. Pine shavings littered the top where Boss Hog once lived, leaving an outline of the cage.

"When you're done," Big Jack said, "come help me out in the garage. We got a lotta shit to do."

"Yes, sir."

When his father was gone, Jack took out four sets of underwear and socks, dumping them onto the bed. From the closet, he took down a nylon bag. He drew up his nose at the smell from the closet, where a small hatch led to the underside of the house. He didn't understand the purpose of the hatch, but it gave way to the muddy underbelly of the house, broken up by sections of concrete slab. Wood roaches and other bugs sometimes crawled up out of the hatch and an earthy, drainage ditch smell emanated from the closet at all times.

Jack grabbed his hiking boots and gathered a few other things, including some jeans and t-shirts, then piled everything on the bed next to the duffel bag.

Big Jack yelled from the other room. "Pack warm, boy. It's gonna be colder than a witch's titty."

Picking through odd spots in his room, Jack found his pocketknife, canteen and compass. Holding the plastic compass, he tilted it one way then another, watching the bubble move back and forth under the glass. He put the canteen into the bag first, followed by his clothing. After stuffing the socks down around everything else, he laid the compass and the knife on top and zipped up the duffel bag. From the lowest shelf in the closet, he took down a shoebox filled with trading cards, each bearing a classic movie monster. Among the cards, he located his flashlight, a Christmas gift from his great grandmother. She had grown up in a house without electricity and placed great value in having a flashlight handy. His father had attached a silver chain to one end and a set of pewter deer antlers hung from the chain. As he often did, Jack held the flashlight like the haft of a weapon and spun the antlers around in a circle until they were a blur of metallic teeth at the end of the beaded chain. He tucked the flashlight into his bag and carried it out.

Big Jack was standing in the center of the garage with gear and baggage scattered around him. He was holding a rolled up camouflage poncho in one hand. The garage door was open and the truck was backed up to the eaves of the house, tailgate down. Eyeing Jack's bag, he said, "That all you got?"

"Yeah," Jack said.

"Good. Travelin' light...like a man. If your momma was going she'd be taking half this house." Big Jack stuffed the poncho into the top of an ice chest and closed the lid. He lit a cigarette, surveying the garage and prodding a fluorescent lantern with the toe of his boot, dimpled ostrich skin. It was his habit to change boots after work.

Jack stood near the wall, leaning on the unpainted sheet rock.

Big Jack took a drag on his cigarette and said, "Let's see... we don't need no fishin' gear, since this is a huntin' trip." He laughed. "Alright, I'm bringing the tent, just in case, but we probably ain't gonna need it. They got a pretty good lodge up there." He rambled along, ignoring Jack until he turned and said, "Okay, boy...why don't you load all this up into the truck, starting up near the cab. I'll throw a tarp over it and lash it down before we take off in the morning. Alright?"

"Yes, sir." He set about moving things into the back of the truck, starting with his duffel bag.

After watching him for a moment, Big Jack dropped his cigarette and stepped on it. "Goddamn, I love deer season." He turned and went into the house.

"Get up, boy...time to go."

Jack woke up just before five in the morning with his father shaking him roughly. He rolled over, trying to shake off sleep. Most mornings, it was hard enough for him to get up in time for school. On the rare occasions when he woke up this early, his head felt like it was filled with pins and needles. He squinted against the light from the hallway.

Big Jack said, "I'll be in the garage."

The house was quiet. Jack rested on his pillow, feeling heavy. His eyes rolled back in his head and he was asleep again after a few breaths.

When Big Jack stepped back into the doorway a short time later, surprise and anger flashed across his face as he looked down at the boy, sleeping. "Goddammit...get the fuck up." Though he wasn't yelling, he spoke the words with such tightly-packed hostility that they cut through his son's sleep.

Jack sprang up, blinking and shaking his head. His mouth was wide open and an animal whimper escaped before he clamped down on it. Only five minutes had passed, but it felt like an hour.

"If you wanna go on this trip," Big Jack said, "you better get your ass out of bed."

Jack conformed to the fiction, playing the role of the son who wanted to go hunting with his father. "I'm up."

"Alright," Big Jack said, nodding and eyeing him from the doorway. "You oughta eat something. Once I get rollin', I ain't stoppin'." He left the room again, heading down the hall.

Alone again, Jack pushed himself up and sat at the edge of the bed, slumped over. He closed his eyes and opened them wide several times. He stood up and struggled out of his t-shirt and striped socks, leaving them where they fell next to the bed. Padding down the hall to the bathroom, his head still ached but he started to shake off his stupor.

Jack turned the shower knobs, adjusting the water temperature. Standing at the sink, he brushed his teeth while the room filled with steam. He left the toothbrush on the counter so he'd remember it, then stretched out on the bathroom rug, spat into his hand, and jerked off. Afterward, he showered quickly.

Back in his room, he put on a flannel shirt, dressing for the long drive. He walked to the kitchen, started some toast and poured a bowl of chocolate cereal. Wind buffered the screened window over the sink as he stood at the counter, spooning up the cereal. When the toast popped up, he stacked both pieces on a paper towel and buttered them. He ate the toast and finished the cereal in silence.

Big Jack came into the kitchen from the garage. "You 'bout ready?" He refilled his coffee mug from the pot next to the refrigerator.

"Yeah," Jack said. He cleaned up the crumbs from his toast and started to rinse his cereal bowl in the sink.

"Leave that for your momma," Big Jack said, "...whenever she decides to get her lazy ass outta bed." He walked into the living room.

Jack finished up at the sink, listening to the house. It was quiet, except for the hum of the refrigerator. As he passed the door to the garage, he could see the early colors of the sun through the open garage door, making the sky glow above the houses across the street. Their rooftops stood out, black against the dawn and they sat like low monuments. Higher up, the last span of night was cobalt. His father's truck sat in the driveway, with their gear piled under a tarp. A car passed as a neighbor headed for an early morning shift.

BIG JACK is DEAD

In the living room, Big Jack stood near the gun cabinet, which housed the key components of the hunting trip. The tall upper section was glass. The base featured carved wooden doors, inlaid with fake mother-of-pearl. Inside, there were cartons of ammo and cleaning rags. When the doors were open, the living room smelled of gunpowder. Two shotguns and a .22 caliber rifle stood upright in the gun cabinet. Big Jack had removed his new Weatherby, along with his older rifle, which Jack would use over the weekend. Long traveling cases for the rifles lay on the carpet, unzipped and spread open like narrow sleeping bags. The older rifle rested on one of the felt-lined cases. The other traveling case lay empty.

Aiming through the front windows, Big Jack held the Weatherby against his shoulder, scanning up and down the block through the scope.

This was something he did each year around hunting season, sighting in on pedestrians, neighborhood dogs and the people driving down the block. He chuckled as he trained the rifle on a man pulling out of his driveway in a battered pickup. "Henry's pickin' his goddamn nose on the way out to the plant." Tracking the pickup, he breathed loudly through his mouth. "He's a little squirrelly."

He looked back over his shoulder at Jack, who stood like a spook at the farthest end of the room. "This scope is still perfectly sighted," Big Jack said with an air of awe for the weapon. "Still goddamn sighted, months after the last time I shot it."

"I can't believe it," Jack said, feigning amazement.

"Well, you better…this is the best fuckin' rifle a man can own."

"Yes, sir." He shielded his eyes against the rays of dawn coming through the window.

Big Jack knelt on the carpet and eased his rifle into the case. He zipped the bag, tracing the outline of the weapon and enfolding it snugly in canvas and cloth. "Alrighty," he said. "Let's get these bad boys into the truck." He picked up the case and slung the strap across his chest. He stood looking at Jack. "You're growin' up, boy. You're big enough to carry your own gun now, so get it."

Jack zipped up his rifle and hung it from his shoulder.

"Let's go." Big Jack's eyes were alive with an eerie eagerness, but he whirled at the last second. "Goddamn, almost forgot." He returned to the gun cabinet, retrieving his nine millimeter pistol from a lower shelf. "Gotta have this for the road," he said, winking at his son, "…in case we get jumped by niggers." He closed up the cabinet and the truck keys jangled in his hand as he turned the lock. "Let's go, boy. We got a lot of driving to do."

Weapon slung over his back, Jack followed his father to the garage. As he pulled the garage door down and twisted the handle, he wished his mother had come to say goodbye.

Big Jack stowed the rifles over the rear window, maneuvering around in the cab on his knees, causing the springs in the seat to groan and grind as he shifted his weight. He checked the ropes holding the tarp one last time, cackling like some mad Santa inspecting his sled. Satisfied, he pulled himself up behind the wheel just as Jack was climbing into the passenger seat.

"Alright, boy," Big Jack said. "Let's hit the goddamn road."

Still sleepy, Jack watched through the windshield as the houses on his block slipped past.

In keeping with one of his rituals, Big Jack stopped for chocolate milk and doughnuts at the onset of the hunting trip. Tichacek's was popular with his fellow plant-workers, who frequented the place several times a week on the way to work. Hopping down out of the truck, he hitched up his pants, which were immediately dragged low again by the large knife now hanging from his belt. He spat into the parking lot. "Keep an eye on the truck. I'll be right back."

Jack watched his father enter and pass along the front window. A long bar stretched the length of the room, where men sat on stools. Most of them were dressed in the same attire his father put on five mornings a week. Waitresses drifted around, filling up coffee cups and bringing out plates of fried eggs, bacon and sausage, delivering them to the tables scattered through the restaurant. One end of the bar was reserved for patrons picking up batches of doughnuts in paper bags.

Big Jack leaned on the counter, chatting with the plump waitress taking his order. He wore a camouflage jacket with a hood over his t-shirt. The inner lining of the jacket was bright orange, like a traffic cone. The camo was supposed to prevent deer from seeing him by breaking up his outline; the orange lining was supposed to prevent other hunters from shooting him to death by mistake.

After he paid, the waitress passed him a couple of bags. They talked for a few more minutes before he headed for the exit. The bells on the front of the shop jingled as he emerged. Sitting in the truck, he and Jack ate a couple of doughnuts each and drank from half-pint containers of chocolate milk.

"Those fuckers are jealous I'm goin' hunting." He cackled, with flakes of sugar raining down from his whiskered lips. Jack laughed with him. The windows fogged up, so Big Jack started the engine and cranked the defroster to max.

"That's Shirley," he said, once the glass was clear again. Through the windshield, he indicated the woman who had waited on him. "She's a pretty good ol' girl." He looked at his son confidentially. "She likes me a lot."

Unsure of what to say, Jack smiled and tore off another chunk of doughnut.

The ride out to the deer lease was long. Leaving the Gulf Coast behind, they moved into the stark, gray-green landscape of East Texas; sparse pastures dotted with long-faced cattle, scrubby woods and endless highways flanked by barbed wire. They passed through dying towns, composed mostly of feed stores, traffic lights and gas stations. Big Jack chain-smoked throughout the drive. Occasionally, he listened to the truck's AM radio, tuning in some country music station. He left it on through the first half of a high school football game, re-broadcast from earlier in the season, before the signal finally failed.

Jack felt nauseous, breathing the cigarette smoke, but the air was too chilly to leave the windows down. He stared out the windshield most of the time. Beyond the glass, the world was a blur. After a few hours, he retrieved another doughnut from the white paper bag, careful to leave one in case his father wanted it.

They stopped for lunch at a Dairy Queen in Halletsville. Sitting in a booth, they drank Dr. Pepper from Styrofoam cups.

Big Jack pointed to one of the cups. "We make this shit, you know…" He dipped a steak finger into a small tub of gravy then into the pool of ketchup next to his French fries, leaving a milky blot in the ketchup.

Jack looked surprised. "Y'all make Dr. Pepper at the plant?"

"No, goddammit, boy. We make the stuff that the cups are made out of…" His eyes rolled up in his head as he gestured across the room. "None of these people would be drinking these Cokes if we didn't make the goddamn Styrofoam." He stuffed the steak finger into his mouth and chewed.

Jack nodded and pretended to study the cup in awe. Watching his father across the tabletop, he took a bite of his enormous burger. The Dairy Queen dining room was surrounded by windows. Sitting next to the glass, there was a chill and he pulled his jacket closer to his body.

BIG JACK is DEAD

Alternating between fries dipped in ketchup and his burger, which was smothered in mustard, Jack's mouth was awash in salty, tangy tastes. Periodically, he slugged down a few gulps of his Dr. Pepper to rinse it all away. A few people left the dining room and a puff of cold air pushed its way across the table. Eventually, he opened up the cup, tearing the plastic lid off and munching on the crushed ice.

When they were done, Big Jack went to the counter and ordered a cup of coffee to go.

Jack went into the restroom and locked the door. He peed and splashed water on his face at the sink. Someone had scratched a girlfriend's name into the mirror and someone else had written "sucks dicks" in black marker on the wall next to it. Reading the words gave Jack an erection. He stood there for as long as he thought he could, enjoying the privacy. Relaxed, he leaned into the counter top and studied his face in the scarred mirror before rejoining his father in the truck.

"I thought you must've fell in," Big Jack said. The engine took a while to get going and then they moved out onto the narrow highway.

It was roughly noon when they reached the lease and the temperature had dropped sharply. The sky was bright and clear, with cottony clouds stretching across the vastness. A dirt road ran from the highway, leading deeper into the property. Eaten away by flash floods, the grade was uneven, pitching the truck from side to side. They turned several times onto smaller roads, following a course that Big Jack seemed to intuit his way through.

When they stopped at a gate, he sat behind the wheel while his son went out to open the gate, in keeping with an age-old Texas ritual. Standing in the cold, Jack braced against the wind. He un-looped a chain and walked the gate open. It squeaked as it swung out. He searched the corrugated aluminum for a handhold free of spider webs and held the gate in place as the truck rolled forward. The tires crunched on the gravel road then buzzed like tank treads in a war movie as they hit the parallel pipes of the cattle guard. Once his father had driven through, Jack walked the gate closed and re-looped the chain. He trotted over to the truck and jumped into the passenger seat, hurrying to get out of the cold. As he slammed the door, Jack and his father grinned at one another, excited by the temperature. The wind whistled against the triangular windows near the dash.

"This is huntin' weather," Big Jack said.

Half a mile later, they arrived at the lodge, an old house standing in a stretch of prairie. The paint had long since peeled away, leaving the place bleached and ghostly. Bloody streaks of rust marked the tin roof and an open porch wrapped like a jawbone around two sides. In varying states of disrepair, mismatched lawn chairs were scattered along the porch.

Swinging around in a fishhook arc, Big Jack pulled up to the rear of the house and killed the truck. A fire-blackened barrel stood a dozen yards from the back door in a ring of scorched earth. The house sat on blocks and no step led down from the back door. It just dropped.

"Goddamn, finally here. I work all year long for this shit." Through knee high grass, he walked to the house with his hands jammed into his jacket pockets. His boots echoed as he stepped up onto the porch. Looking out across the prairie, he studied the stark landscape while the wind moaned through a jagged hole in the overhang of the tin roof.

Closing the door to the truck as quietly as he could, Jack leaned into it until the latch popped. As he came closer to his father, the wooden floor creaked, flexing under his weight. Following the direction of his father's gaze, he looked across the expanse and wiped his nose on his sleeve.

"Two thousand acres," Big Jack said quietly. He dropped his cigarette and turned back to the house. The spring on the screen door produced a long, rusty yawning, like a piano dying. He handed the door off to Jack and turned the antique ceramic knob. They entered the old house and stood just inside, looking around. The place was used only once each year for hunting season. It smelled like an attic, the odors of someplace once inhabited by people but now the domain of mice. Several couches and a ripped recliner sat in the living room. Situated at the far end of the structure, the kitchen gave access to the back door and its perilous drop. Several bedrooms and a single bathroom opened up off the living room. With each step, the floor groaned like the timbers of a ship.

"Let's get a fire going," Big Jack said. "Then we can unpack." He went over to the stove and inspected it, rattling the cold porcelain grates. "Gotta light the goddamn pilot..." He flipped on the gas and looked around before discovering the pilot light underneath. Crouching then rolling over onto his side, he struggled to get a wooden kitchen match lit before reaching in deeper beneath the stove, blindly attempting to ignite the gas.

A sheet of flame emerged from beneath the stove. Wide-eyed, Jack watched as it rolled around his father and across the wooden floor, moving slowly, as if someone had overturned a bathtub. It stopped a foot short of Jack.

BIG JACK is DEAD

Big Jack screamed as the flames flowed past him. "LORD GOD!" He jumped up and shook his head like a dog emerging from a lake. Bringing his hands up to touch his face, he ran them over his whiskers, patting himself. "Holy shit, boy." Doubled over, he blinked and exhaled hard. "I didn't know it'd do that."

Jack saw that it was okay, that his father was smiling, so he chuckled. His father rarely hit him any more, but his brooding anger and outbursts kept Jack wary. "That was squirrelly," Jack said. "But kind of cool, too."

The two of them went back outside and started unpacking, moving their gear into two of the bedrooms. After a couple of loads, they took a break in the kitchen, standing at the stove, warming themselves. Watching his father as he held his hands over the flames, Jack remembered Boss Hog. Sadness rose up within him and he went back outside, into the cold.

Carrying in the last load from the truck, Jack walked around in the room he'd chosen before dropping his bag. There were a few beds set up in both rooms, including some bunks with rusty frames. The place could sleep up to eight or more people, depending on whether anyone shared a bed.

On a windowsill in his room, Jack found a ten inch centipede, dead and long-desiccated. He let his eyes take it in then prodded the red-brown husk, made up of wide, flat segments. Losing interest, he turned away and hefted his bag up onto the bed.

Big Jack called out from the next room. "The others oughta be here in an hour or two."

Jack stopped moving, listening closely.

"...John-David is coming and Ricky. They're bringing their boys, so you'll have someone your own age to shoot the shit with."

Jack closed his eyes and his stomach lurched. He knew these kids. They were four or five years older. He remembered them holding him underwater in a drainage ditch, forcing him down until he went wild with panic, thrashing like an animal. They only let him up after he inhaled a lungful of muddy water. Lying on the wet grass, he choked for ten minutes. Another time, they wrapped him in duct tape and sprayed roach killer into his eyes. "Great," he called out.

Once they were settled, Big Jack started a pot of coffee and the two of them sat on the porch. Jack broke sticks into smaller pieces and dropped them at his feet in a pile while his father chain-smoked, throwing the butts of his cigarettes off the front end of the porch. They peered across the tawny open space stretching before them.

Staring at the same patch of dry grass, Jack saw nothing of interest at first, until he realized that he was looking at a jackrabbit. One moment it was just dead grass and brambles, the next the unmistakable form of a jackrabbit. It crouched, its fur so perfectly matching the colorless prairie that the rabbit was almost invisible. The wind blew through the field and he whispered to his father, "Look at that jackrabbit."

"Where?" Big Jack was excited and childlike.

Jack pointed, directing his father's eyes to the right.

"I see it," Big Jack said. He licked his lips. "I oughta go get my rifle."

Jack blinked hard and his pointing hand dropped a few inches. He watched the rabbit, unsure of how to respond. It stood upright then froze, holding the position with dead-serious patience.

His father shifted his chair backward and the jackrabbit took off in a blur of gray and tan, vanishing into the windblown grass. Big Jack chuckled softly. "Yeah, you little motherfucker, you better run." He spat toward the edge of the porch and nearly made it.

Jack watched the spot in the field where the rabbit had been, saying a prayer for it without words.

A few hours later, after they'd eaten a few sandwiches made from potted meat and Wonder bread, Jack cocked his head. "Someone's coming up the road." They walked to the back door and dropped down into the dirt behind the house as two more trucks pulled up.

"Well, goddamn," Big Jack said. "John-David got himself a new truck." With reverence in his eyes, he turned to look at his son. "Look at that goddamn thing."

John-David and Ricky were in the first truck, the newer one. Their sons were stuffed into the second. At seventeen, the oldest of the boys was driving. Pulling up in a cloud of dust, both vehicles stopped near Big Jack's battered black truck. All four doors opened at once and slammed together after everyone piled out.

"Goddamn," Ricky yelled. "It's fuckin' huntin' season." He was short, but heavily muscled. His hair was the color of dirty straw and his beard was curly.

John-David was a great hog of a man. Over six and a half feet tall and enormous in girth, he loomed over the others. "Yessir," he said, coming around from the driver's side. "Yessir, it is at that." He tugged on his checkered baseball cap and swung one of his legs out, adjusting his balls. "Y'all boys unload the truck."

"Help 'em," Big Jack added without turning to his son.

The three men gathered and shook hands near the rusted barrel.

"Man, I like that truck," Big Jack said.

"Yeah, it's nice," John-David said. "It'll haul a fucking ton, too."

Ricky rubbed his face thoughtfully, pulling down on his beard. "How's the place look?"

"Oh, it's alright," Big Jack said. "Kitchen's kind of small…"

Ricky furrowed his brow and looked at Big Jack with disbelief. "Not the house, dipshit…the lease." Ricky and John-David both laughed at Big Jack, who looked uncertain for a second then laughed along with them.

"Oh," Big Jack said. "We ain't seen no deer yet."

John-David bobbed his head up and down a few times. "Alright then, let's drink some goddamn beer."

Carrying some of the gear from Ricky's truck, Jack walked along with the older boys. They clomped across the wooden floors of the old house, filling the place with noise. In the cramped bedroom, they threw their bundles down onto the bunks and headed out for another load.

As the boys passed through the kitchen, John-David, Ricky and Big Jack were dividing up the deer lease, each laying claim to a compass direction. The three of them were huddled over a map spread across the rickety kitchen table. The map of the property had been folded and unfolded so many times that it was more like cloth than paper, and the corners had frayed away, leaving cross-shaped holes.

"I'll take the northwest side," John-David said. The north end constituted the largest section of the property. It was lush with the thickets favored by whitetail deer.

Ricky dug a wad of snuff from between his teeth and gums. "I got the east, then," he said. "I've hunted it before."

John-David and Ricky looked at each other for a second after staking out their respective domains. Both of them nodded and they turned to Big Jack.

He blinked at the map then looked up at each of them, chewing on a mouthful of potted meat sandwich. Crumbs fell from his whiskered face and his eyes were full of wariness. The south end of the property was the smallest and had the least tree coverage. A series of gullies ran like stretch marks across the surface of the land there where the property line came up against a dairy farm.

"I'll fight you sons of bitches tooth and nail for the south side," he said.

Opening a beer, John-David smirked. "We just told you we want the north side and the east side..."

BIG JACK is DEAD

"Well all right then," Big Jack said. "There ain't no dispute."

After carrying in the last of the gear from the trucks, the boys gathered in the bunk room. Jack leaned the backpack he was carrying against the wall. They all stood near the middle of the room.

"This place is a fucking dump," Mike said. He was the youngest of Ricky's sons. Pulling a knife from his belt, he threw it down in front of him. It stuck hard and stood eight inches tall, embedded in the worn wood.

His older brother, Brandon, laughed. "We oughta take the truck out tonight and go back up to that Girl Scout camp we went past...get some pussy."

John-David's son Kohen pushed him. "You wouldn't know what to do with pussy if pussy found you."

"Bullshit...more than you, queer."

The three older boys continued to laugh and trade insults. At twelve, Jack was much slighter and stood a foot shorter. He stood in silence, trying to avoid notice. He wanted to leave the room, but knew that he couldn't without drawing attention.

Mike, who was fifteen, picked up the knife. A wild, challenging look came into his eyes. He spotted the centipede husk and speared it with the tip of the knife. Rapt, they all stared at the centipede, which was almost a foot long.

"That thing's nearly as big as my dick," Kohen said.

Brandon scowled. "You wish, mother-fucker."

Surprising everyone, Mike flicked the knife, sending the centipede flying at Jack, who barely dodged it. Everyone else burst into fits of laughter.

Jack stomped the shit out of it as it landed, crushing the brittle thing into pieces on the wooden floor. Somehow this action saved him from further hostility. He knew better than to cave in or to whine, but he also knew that fighting back would require Mike to put him on the ground.

"Can you imagine that thing crawlin' up your ass in the middle of the night," Jack said. Everyone laughed hard. Looking up, he could see that they approved. Even Mike was laughing, his face twisted into perverse knots as he thought about the centipede clawing its way past his anus.

Standing nearly as tall as his father, Kohen headed toward the door. "Let's go get the rest of this shit 'fore daddy has a fucking conniption fit."

That night they all gathered in back around the trash barrel. The boys carried chairs from the porch, arranging them in a chaotic semi-circle around the barrel. Everyone bundled up against the cold and they all looked thicker in their layers of clothing. Ricky started a fire in the barrel, using some old porn magazines, a pile of firewood and a few cups of gasoline. At first the blaze flared up to twice the height of the barrel, causing them all to back up and lighting up the back side of the old house.

"Fucking cool," Mike said.

After the fire calmed, Jack sat on a folding stool and watched the sparks rise from the mouth of the barrel. Peering through holes rusted into the side, he could see deep into the white-hot center of the burning wood.

The men drank Lone Star beer from bottles and the boys drank Mr. Pibb from cans.

Ricky asked, "What kind of deer you gonna get, J.D.?"

John-David spat. "I figure a ten, maybe a twelve point buck."

"My ass," Ricky said. "Maybe a spike..." He chuckled good-naturedly.

A spike was a male deer with simple antlers that rose like twin digits of bone, instead of branching out like many-fingered hands.

"If you see a spike," Big Jack said, "You gotta shoot it even if it takes up your last huntin' tag." He looked sternly at his son as if passing along some key wisdom.

"Yep," Ricky said. "You gotta get it out of the breedin' pool. Ain't worth much, but you gotta do it."

Tilting back a beer, Big Jack turned to John-David. "I never heard nobody call you J.D.," he said.

"Well, some do," John-David said.

"It sounds good," Big Jack said. "Funny how it only works with some names."

Trying to join the conversation, Jack said, "Works with Big Jack."

"Yeah," said Ricky with a wicked grin, "it does…B.J."

Big Jack looked at Ricky then smiled at his son and laughed. "Yeah…got a good ring to it, don't it? Just like J.D."

"Uh-huh," Jack said. He took a sip of cold Mr. Pibb.

"Well-sir," John-David said. "I'll tell you what…" They all looked at him. "I sure could use me a B.J. about right now if the old lady was around and if she was drunk enough to let me put it in her mouth."

Working out his meaning, everyone was silent. Then they laughed together and turned their eyes on Big Jack.

Suddenly he looked malevolent and flustered. "I do believe I'd slap the shit outta anyone who went around calling me B.J.," he said, staring at his son.

BIG JACK is DEAD

The wind whipped up and the fire burned hotter. It crackled and sent up more sparks. Jack swallowed and gazed into the fire.

"Daddy?" Kohen said.

John-David occupied the largest of the chairs, a metal rocking chair that had required two of the boys to move it from the porch. The chair groaned against his weight each time he shifted in place. "Yeah?"

"You mind if we take one of the trucks out to Q-beam some rabbits?"

"I don't," John-David said, "But you sure as fuck ain't taking my new truck."

"You ain't taking mine either," Ricky said. He knocked back the last of his beer and threw the bottle into the barrel, sending another column of sparks racing up into the dark sky. He reached for another beer.

"Take mine," Big Jack said. "It's old." His eyes got fierce. "But don't you fucking wreck it."

Kohen nodded once. "I won't, sir."

"My boy's too small to drive it," Big Jack said. There was an apologetic note in his voice. "Y'all take him out there and scare some of the pussy out of him." Everyone laughed hard, surprising Big Jack. Cutting his eyes to one side, he realized they were laughing at his son and felt relief. He laughed along with them, fishing out his truck keys and throwing them toward Kohen, where they landed in the dirt at his feet.

Glaring at Big Jack, Kohen reached down and picked up the keys. "Thank you, sir." He finished off his Mr. Pibb and tossed the can into the fire. "Let's go, then."

The boys headed into the house to get their rifles. Jack got to his feet and followed. They regrouped at the truck, geared up to go. Kohen climbed in behind the wheel and Brandon slid into the passenger's side. Mike and Jack stood in the bed of the truck holding onto the network of metal pipes welded into place over the back window and around the top of the cab. Big Jack had intended to mount running lights there, but never got around to finishing the task.

Kohen started the engine and took off cautiously, navigating out onto the dirt road. The truck flattened clumps of weeds then crunched along in the gravel, the headlights illuminating the scrub brush ahead. Once he was far enough away from the house, he stomped the gas, taking the truck down into a sloping ditch and into a level field beyond. The truck almost threw the boys standing in the back as it lurched along, the toolbox at Jack's feet rattling with every bump.

BIG JACK is DEAD

Working against the turbulence, Brandon plugged the pigtail cord of the Q-beam spotlight into the cigarette lighter. He flicked the switch and a white sun lit up the cab of the truck. Brandon laughed as he directed the thing across the field. He held it by the rubberized pistol-grip, intoxicated by its brightness, which measured in hundreds of thousands of candlepower. The beam was so intense that it projected a harsh, white line out into the night air for a great distance. As it passed through the brush and the branches, it created shadows like the tangled legs of a million insects.

Jack turned to the older boy next to him and smiled. "This is huntin' weather."

Mike didn't turn. "Yeah, colder than shit."

A few miles further, Kohen slowed the engine. Brandon pointed the Q-beam out the window into the field, scanning the landscape. Mike prepared his rifle, resting it on top of the cab of the truck.

When Brandon finally spotted a jackrabbit, everyone went quiet and Kohen braked the truck, idling in place while Mike aimed. The rabbit stood frozen in a circle of light. When the shot went off, Jack flinched and Brandon let out a warlike cry. The rabbit jumped six feet into the air and came down flailing and thrashing.

After the older boys stopped yelling, Jack could hear a wailing sound. It sounded like a baby crying. Squinting in discomfort, he asked, "What the fuck is that?"

"I just winged it," Mike said. "Rabbit's cry like that...you ain't never heard it?"

"No." Jack wanted to shut out the sound, which was terrible. Out in the field, the jackrabbit writhed on its side, arching its head backward unnaturally far. Its powerful hind legs pawed the air as some part of it tried to run. It continued to emit the keening sound. "Aren't you going to shoot it again?" Jack asked.

"Why?" Mike seemed disturbed by the question. "It ain't goin' nowhere." He looked back out into the field, following the Q-beam as his brother swept it through the grass.

"There's another one," Brandon called out from inside the cab. Kohen allowed the truck to creep forward and Mike readied himself for another shot.

They continued for another hour, shooting twelve rabbits in all. The older boys took turns at the rifle and manning the Q-beam, but Jack refused. The others looked at him with disdain, but were more than happy to take his turns. He crouched down low in the bed of the truck, huddling against the metal and wrapping himself up tighter in his jacket. The air grew more damp and the cold was bitter.

When they returned to the house, the men were all drunk and greeted the boys wildly. Jack came close to the fire barrel for warmth, but it had mostly gone out.

"You have fun?" Big Jack asked him.

"Yes, sir," Jack said.

The combined effects of drunkenness and exhaustion set in and everyone grew quiet. A morose, hostile atmosphere settled over the group.

Jack slipped away from the circle of men and boys, creeping off to the bedroom. The house was unheated and had grown colder in the night. He turned off the light and got into bed. Even wearing his clothes and wrapped in a sleeping bag, it was still freezing. He drifted off to sleep, wrestling in his mind with Mike. He replayed the day's incident with the centipede, but added to it. He saw himself driving the boy's knife up through the bottom of his jaw at the base of his throat and into his skull. These were his last waking thoughts as he fell into sleep.

Big Jack shook him awake a few hours later. Everyone else was already up and dressing, moving around sluggishly in the frigid, pre-dawn air of the house. Most of the lights were still out and occasionally someone cursed bitterly. Jack dressed and met his father in the front room.

Big Jack was drinking coffee and smoking. He was wearing camouflage clothing from head to foot. He looked at his son harshly. "Where's your goddamn gun, boy?"

Still in a stupor, Jack went back into the bedroom and took his hand-me-down rifle off the gun rack. He also retrieved a pair of gloves from his duffel bag. He folded them together before slipping them into his pocket, doubling them over like socks.

Back in the front room, his father looked him over while sipping hot coffee from a thermos. "Alright...let's go."

After warming up the truck, Big Jack drove south across the property. Jack fell asleep a few times, jolting awake whenever his father hit a rock or pothole.

Big Jack stopped the truck near an open gate just before dawn. He'd been driving very slowly and whispered when he spoke, operating in a kind of silent-running mode. He pointed into the woods along the fence line. "You follow that bob wire for a piece...couple hundred yards. You'll come to an orange stand. That's yours."

Jack nodded. He felt unnerved by the notion of heading out into the woods alone while it was still dark.

"You got toilet paper?" Big Jack asked.

Taken by surprise, Jack looked down at his lap. "No, sir."

"Well goddamn, boy. You wanna wipe your ass with a stick?"

"No, sir."

"Take some of mine then." Big Jack reached over and opened up the glove box. He removed a roll of toilet paper that had been crushed flat and unwound a section that was four feet long. He wadded it up and handed it to Jack, who stuffed it into a side pocket on his jacket.

"Alright then," Big Jack said. "You need anything, like a 'mergency, shoot in the air three times." He paused, inhaling from his cigarette and studying his son. "Too cold for snakes, so you'll be okay."

Jack opened the door and took his rifle down from the back window of the truck. He stepped away, out onto the edge of the dirt road and quietly shut the door, knowing not to slam it.

"I'll be back around lunch. Wish me luck, boy."

"Good luck," Jack said, but the truck pulled away as he spoke. The scarlet taillights receded as his father braked and took the truck around a bend, vanishing from sight. Soon even the engine, mostly idling along, was too quiet to hear. Jack turned and made his way off the crumbling dirt road and into the brush, hugging the barbed wire fence. Walking along, he tugged on his gloves against the cold.

When he reached the towering deer stand, he propped his rifle against a nearby tree. Searching around in the dark, he found a stick that was over a foot in length then climbed the ladder leading up into the stand, eight feet off the ground. With the stick and his small flashlight, he cleared away spider webs and searched the underside of the tall chair installed next to the window. Careful to make as little noise as possible, he wadded up the silver chain attached to the end of the flashlight and held it in his palm, the pewter antlers biting into his flesh.

When he was confident that there were no spiders, wasps or scorpions in the stand, he threw the stick off into the grass and climbed back down to the ground. He detested bugs with a fury and took no chances, even though it was really too cold for insects. He slung his rifle over one shoulder and climbed the ladder again.

It was still too dark to see, so he propped the rifle in one corner of the stand and settled into the chair. Long, low windows surrounded him on all sides. He looked out into the darkness, barely able to make out the black fields beyond. For a time, he imagined himself a sniper, waiting for the president's motorcade. Eventually, he settled back in the chair and fell asleep.

BIG JACK is DEAD

When he opened his eyes, the world was lit with gray light, allowing him to see through the scrub brush surrounding the stand. A lonely mesquite tree stood fifty yards away at the left end of a field and a dozen whitetail deer stood scattered around the tree. Jack blinked a few times and felt sleep fall away from him. He stared at the deer and licked his lips in the cold.

In the morning light, the color of their coats was one part autumn leaves, one part fireplace ash. They blended against the dead grass and cold dirt beneath them, standing like forest spirits around the twisted mesquite.

Breathless and quiet, he eased forward and put one hand on his rifle, lifting it without knocking it against the stand. In his mind, he saw his father laughing with glee, clapping him on the shoulder. Jack rotated the gun around with both hands until the barrel pointed out through the front window, parallel with the cold ground. Feeling with his sneakers, he positioned his feet on the lowest rung under the chair and pushed himself to the edge of his seat. He pulled the stock into his shoulder, his body settling down around the rifle, leaning against the window frame. Making a few small adjustments, he looked through the scope, out across the field.

At first his eyes focused on a spot far beyond the herd. He swept the barrel down by a few inches and the ground rushed by like the waters of a fast-moving river, many yards passing in a second. He settled on a doe, standing in perfect profile. The cross hairs were as fine as the legs of a wasp and Jack put them over her heart. His own heart flipped in his chest like a fish as he struggled to stay calm. Running on autopilot, he wanted to do everything right, everything perfect. He held his breath and squeezed the trigger slowly as his father had taught him.

The report of the rifle destroyed the tranquility of the field. Jack didn't even feel the gun kick against his shoulder. He lifted his eye from the rubber circle of the scope and watched as the deer raced toward the brush line like a pack of perfect athletes. The herd moved like the downward flow of water, all save one. The doe lay on the ground as the others fled.

Relaxing, he released his breath in a steamy burst. His nose was running and the tip was cold, so he wiped it on the forearm of his coat. Calm settled over him as he studied the field.

Her adrenaline might enable her to get up and run if he approached now. He knew stories, practically since birth, about wounded deer running for miles or turning on hunters and goring them. Peering through the scope again, he watched as she kicked on the ground, still moving, but not as much as he had expected. The hole in her shoulder faced up to the sky and was dark, barely noticeable. Eventually she was completely still. With the other deer gone, he felt alone with her in the field. Another five minutes passed. Sometimes he lifted his head to look out across the field where nothing moved.

As he climbed from the stand and crossed the field, he hunched forward against the cold wind that pushed itself across the open terrain. The rifle hung over his right shoulder as he approached, almost as long as he was tall. The ground was wet with dew, but was not quite frozen. A damp trail stretched out behind him in the grass, leading back to the stand.

His mind reeled when he drew near the mesquite tree where the doe lay. Having only been close to horses and cows, the deer was tinier than expected, her body more delicate.

I killed a baby, he thought.

His heart went cold and his head felt light as he imagined his father's rage. He could visualize Big Jack's expression and he saw the others back at the camp house laughing at him, berating him for breaking some primal rule of hunting.

He knelt beside the body, resting utterly motionless on its side. His fear faded and tears blinded him as he looked into the black eye of the thing before him, trying and failing to commune with her through the orb that was set like a precious stone in her face. With one hand, he reached out, stroking her fur as he might a sleeping dog. The coarseness surprised him.

"I'm so sorry," he said aloud, wondering at the quietness of his own voice. His breath made fog in the air before him.

Keeping a vigil, Jack sat in the grass next to the doe for a couple of hours until his pants were damp with moisture from the ground and his teeth chattered in his head. Several times, he started crying. Ashamed, he blinked back his tears each time, drying them with his sleeve.

His father's truck came up the road just after eleven. Wiping his eyes a final time, Jack stood and turned toward the approaching sound. The truck door slammed and Big Jack emerged from the brush, smoking as he crossed the field.

"What you got?" he called over the wind.

Jack struggled to keep his throat from closing. "I think I screwed up," he said. He tried to find the right words… something to shift the blame or ameliorate his wrongdoing.

Big Jack drew close. Looking down at the deer, maniacal glee lit up his face. "Goddamn, boy."

"I know," Jack said. "I'm sorry...it looked bigger through the scope." He struggled with his tears as they threatened to return. "I didn't mean to shoot one so young. It was an accident."

In confusion, Big Jack looked up at him. Finally understanding what his son was saying, he shook his head fiercely. "Nuh-uh, boy. What the fuck you thinkin'? That's a doe...they don't get much bigger'n that." Big Jack knelt beside him in the grass and rested one hand on the deer's neck. "You just ain't seen one on the ground like this." He looked at his son closely. "You done real good. This is a good deer...a good kill."

Jack took a breath. "Really?"

"Yeah, oh yeah. I ain't even killed anything yet. You did good." He reached over awkwardly and pawed his son's shoulder then patted him on the back. "Tomorrow I'll probably get an eight or ten point buck, but this is your first year huntin'...a doe ain't bad." Big Jack smiled at him across the body of the fallen animal.

Jack watched his father, soaking in the words. "Okay," he said. "Okay. I just didn't know. It looked so small." He looked back at the deer, pride intermingling with sadness.

Big Jack picked up the doe and slung it over his shoulders, ignoring the thickened blood. Together the two of them walked across the field and into the brush, heading for the truck.

At the end of the weekend, Big Jack drove home from the lease, smoking and staring ahead as the evening hours passed. Occasionally he spoke, offering his son some bit of wisdom as the truck blew along the highway.

"Ain't a lot of people knows this," he said at one point, "but Jesus was a sand nigger." He tilted his head and regarded Jack seriously across the space of the truck. When his son didn't challenge this revelation, Big Jack fell back into a murky, satisfied silence. He gripped the notched steering wheel with one hand, a cigarette poking up between his knuckles.

The trip passed like this, mostly quiet, punctuated by intermittent bits of conversation that randomly brought the boy to alertness, breaking through his daydreams. The ash-green quality of the East Texas landscape gave way to dusky olive then to black as the light fell. The truck finally came off the interstate highway and began to pass through the streets of Lowfield.

Jack was glad for the silence. He was physically exhausted, but also felt a weariness of spirit. The weekend had wrung him out, leaving him drained. He leaned his head against the cold glass of the window, thinking about his favorite comic books and sex, sometimes weaving them together. Cold air leaked around the door of the truck where he leaned against it, licking his right shoulder and his back with a chilly tongue.

The light fixture over the garage door was covered in cobwebs. It cast the truck cab in gold as they came to a stop in the driveway. Jack felt grimy. When he shifted in his layers of clothing, he caught little whiffs of smoke from the fire barrel. Sometimes he smelled something else, which he suspected was blood from the doe.

They got out of the truck and Big Jack opened the garage door. Unloading the bed of the truck, they worked quietly, piling their gear on the garage floor.

Ramona and Brodie came out through the kitchen door.

"Tornado-Bornado, tornado-Bornado, tornado-Bornado." Brodie buzzed along with excitement at their return.

"What'd y'all get?" Ramona asked, smiling. She took a drag from her cigarette and laid her hand firmly on Brodie's shoulder. "Anything? You got deer back there that Brodie can see?"

"I wanna seeee," Brodie whined.

Big Jack drew back his head and straightened his shoulders. "Sure as fuck, we do...you think we went all the way out there to come back with jack shit?" His lighter made a clinking sound as he popped it open with his thumb and deftly lit a cigarette.

The entire family walked to the back end of the pickup truck. Big Jack dropped the tailgate and pulled back the tarp, revealing the bodies of the two slain deer. They lay stretched out on forest-green trash bags. Reaching low, he picked up his youngest son and set him down in the bed of the truck. Brodie's eyes went wide as he looked at the faces of the dead animals a foot away.

Big Jack took the head of the spike buck he had killed and lifted it up. "Look at it, boy." He said the words in the sing-song voice he sometimes used around Brodie. "Your daddy killed a buck...someday you'll get one of these here."

Jack marveled at the black, cloven hooves and the elfin legs. Again he was struck by how delicate the animals were, how ghost-like and fey. He reached out and stroked one of the doe's forelimbs, tracing the coarse fur downward and running his thumb over the dewclaws just below the lowest joint in the foot. The smoke from his parents' cigarettes settled over him as he leaned against the cool metal of the truck. Again, he offered the doe a silent apology.

The plastic trash bags crinkled as Big Jack shifted the head around, holding it by the antlers. Before breaking away, he eyed Jack suspiciously, uncomfortable with his son's demeanor. "Alright, we gotta get this goddamn truck unloaded," he said. "It's late…" He dropped the spike's head and scooped up Brodie, plopping him down onto the driveway.

With her cigarette dangling from her lips, Ramona lifted him to her hips and took him inside, allowing Jack and his father to continue unloading. Squinting as the smoke curled up into her left eye, she mumbled over the cigarette as she moved out of the garage, "I gotta get Brodie into bed."

Carrying his sleeping bag into the center of the garage, Jack watched the kitchen door close at her back. After each armful, he went back for another load, careful to avoid disturbing the bodies of the deer. Passing the length of the truck, he turned his head slightly each time and gazed at the face of the doe, studying her dark, upturned eye.

When the truck was empty and everything was safely inside, Big Jack reached up and closed the garage door with a grunt. The wood and glass rattled and snapped. The metal runners gave a long squeal, thirsty for WD40. Jack flinched as the door boomed down onto the cold concrete floor.

Big Jack slipped a hand into his pocket and pulled out his black and green pocketknife. "Now we gotta cut up this meat," he said.

Chapter 14

1999

People were filling the Communion Hall, a large room decorated in styles from several decades. Black and white tiles covered the floor, worn to gray in places by foot traffic. Everyone mingled or sat in metal folding chairs as they waited for Big Jack's farewell service to start. His body rested elsewhere, in a room dedicated to the funeral ceremony.

My stepmother worked the area, moving among the attendees deftly despite her bulk. I watched her amid the assembly, chatting with each person soberly; shaking hands, hugging and sobbing. She leaned in close to an older woman and whispered something confidential, first looking around dramatically. The older woman reached out and grabbed Mincy's shoulders, holding her a short distance away then hugging her close.

I stood on the back wall, resting against the painted white brick with Brodie. It felt entirely natural to stand with him, despite the occasion, despite the emotional distance between us. It's one of those things from childhood that stays with you. You walk into a room, spot your brother and you go stand next to him. It made me feel better, but at the same time it reminded me that I didn't really know him. Our earlier argument had slipped away; Brodie didn't mention it again and I managed to resist my perverse curiosity. What did it matter if he believed some crazy shit about Dad's death? We stood quietly, watching people enter and mix.

Brodie had fetched our mother an hour earlier, and now she sat alone in a corner, stuck between stupor and grief. She looked out one of the windows blankly, without moving. A steady line of tears ran from her eyes and a trail of shiny mucus stretched from her nostrils to her liver-colored lips. Each time she caught my gaze, I was puzzled; I wasn't sure how to interpret her reaction.

"John-David won't be here, given that he passed away last year," Brodie said.

Suppressing a laugh, I studied my younger brother to see if he was joking. John-David scared the shit out of me as a kid; him and his psychopath sons.

"I guess you knew he had a heart attack."

I narrowed my eyes. "No, I didn't." *And how the fuck would I have known that? It didn't really make the news out West.*

"Yeah, they said it was just an explosive heart attack...out on a deer lease somewhere." He took a sip from the Coke he'd gotten from a vending machine in the funeral home break room. That alone made me laugh. The funeral home sold refreshments. He was so earnest, so disconnected. I wondered what it was like to live anesthetized. "You know he was a big man," he said evenly.

I snorted, unable to help myself. "If by big man you mean morbidly obese ogre, then yes."

Blinking a couple of times, my brother looked at me then at the ground. The lines at the corners of his eyes made him look like he was flinching. He watched my face, surprised at my reaction but finding his nerve. "John-David was a real good friend of Daddy's, you know."

"You're kidding? That's what you think?" I could feel my forehead knotting. Brodie seemed so genuine that it confirmed the existence of a massive delta between our perceptions. "You think they were friends?"

"Hell yeah, I do." His face tensed up; I'd pierced the opiated veil. "They were friends for years, Jack. They hunted together, worked together, drank beer together. He might have been one of Daddy's best friends."

I was at a loss, with no idea what to say. Remembering all the sullen stand-offs, punctuated by moments of cruel humor, I realized that I didn't understand what the word *friend* meant down here. Looking away, I shook my head. "I guess. His friends never made sense to me." But what the fuck did I know? Maybe they had been friends and it was my view of the world that was flawed. Maybe I had no idea what the word friend meant anywhere. Suddenly I wanted to make peace with my brother. "At least John-David died hunting."

He chuckled. "Yeah, true. That's probably what he would have wanted." Indicating a direction with his Coke can, he said, "Kohen is here, his son."

While I was trying to find Kohen in the crowd, an elderly man nearby pointed to Brodie. "That there is his son, one of 'em." Brodie nodded and smiled, walking toward the old man, leaving me alone.

Kohen stood in a corner. He was huge, just as his father had been, over six foot five and fabulously thick. Dressed in a pin-striped suit, he wore wire-frame glasses and fancy cowboy boots. We'd been around each other as kids, but I hadn't seen him in over a decade. Sweat ran from his brow and neck, dampening the dark bristles of his hair. His sideburns were a straggly mass attached to the jowls of his face.

We saw each other across the room and moved closer, shaking hands in the center of the room.

He looked me up and down. "Jack...man, you look good. You still as skinny as you were in high school." He smiled down at me generously, with warmth.

"Thanks, Kohen."

"California is treatin' you right."

I forced myself to smile. "You look good too."

He laughed. "Well, I don't know."

"I appreciate you coming."

"Yessir..." His face became serious. "I felt like I needed to be here, you know. Your daddy was a real good man."

I sucked on my bottom lip for a second, rolling it between my teeth as I remembered my father regarding me with a sharp, avian scrutiny. "Thank you for saying so. It's good to hear that people thought of him that way." As monsters go, he was unbeatable.

"I guess you heard we lost Daddy last year...John-David, I mean."

I ground my teeth together. "Yeah, I was sorry to hear about his passing. Someone I know mentioned it out in Sunnyvale."

Kohen's eyes went wide behind his glasses. "I'll be damned." He blinked a few times.

Resisting the urge to laugh, I nodded. "Your father knew people everywhere. He was well regarded." I studied him, watching his reaction.

Kohen bobbed his chin slowly, looking out over the crowd. He took a deep breath. "Yessir. Yessir, he was. Daddy knew a lot of people and everybody loved him, no matter where he went. He'd done real well at work and out in the world. There were over a hundred people at his funeral." Looking uncomfortable, Kohen cut his head toward me. "Well, goddammit," he said, "I didn't mean nothing by that. I swear I didn't, Jack."

I looked around and tallied the people in the area at probably twenty. Feigning ignorance, I said, "I'm not sure what you mean."

"Oh, I just didn't want you to think that I meant something bad about your daddy. He was a good man. Yessir, he was…"

I studied the room, pausing deliberately. "You mean because there are so few people here?" Turning, I faced him fully. "Is that what you're saying?"

"Aw, lordy, Jack…I'm real sorry for saying that. Sometimes I just say stupid things. That was always Daddy's biggest gripe with me."

I looked at the floor. *You terrified me as a boy, mother-fucker.* "I guess it's true that there aren't many people here...two dozen, if that. He wasn't a great man, Kohen, even though it was nice of you to say that."

He shook his head. "I am so sorry, I really am." Sweating, he reached up and adjusted his collar where it bit into his neck fat.

"I guess that's why he did it," I said, as if the idea was just occurring to me. "He must have known the thing you're talking about...that he wasn't worth much."

Kohen rocked back on his heels. "Lord God, Jack...I wasn't tryin' to infer nothing bad about your daddy."

"No, no...it's okay. Maybe he's better off this way."

"Oh, man, don't say that..."

I regarded him soberly, done with this, wanting to get away. "I'm going to walk around for a while."

He was still distressed. "I feel so stupid, Jack. I am truly sorry."

I smiled up at him, "It's okay. Your dad was a great man and mine was a failure. No one really cared for him. In the end that's why he put his mouth down around the barrel of a pistol and blew out the back of his head."

Kohen looked ashen and clammy.

"Thanks for coming. I'll talk to you later." I walked away from him.

My amusement faded as soon as I left Kohen. With no real connection to anyone here, I didn't know what I was supposed to feel. I moved past the knots of people, pretending not to notice when someone gestured toward me or said my name.

As I passed, someone with a drawl mentioned my father owning a dog. "Yeah, he wrote a hot check for that thing and it was expensive...a bird dog from a breeder up in Montana. But he never did mess with it, so the thing was just half crazy...nearly goddamn dead from starvation when they found it."

The comment made me falter in my step. Head down, I left the Communion Hall. A moment later, I stopped in a corridor outside. Windows ran the length of the passage, bringing in light and making the dingy walls brighter.

There was a drinking fountain in the corridor. The thought of cold water flowing over my face and into my mouth was appealing. My lips were dry and cracked...I needed some kind of relief, some comfort, but I was unable to force myself to drink. The fountain was old, with mineral deposits caked around the spigot. A steady leak ran slowly across the flat aluminum trough and down into the drain. There was a mossy smell emanating from the niche in the wall where the fountain sat. The aged compressor kicked on, filling the hallway with humming and rattling sounds.

I was looking for the break room, but before I could find it, an old man emerged from the restroom and stepped in front of me. He was leaning forward, head down as he toddled along, digging vigorously in one ear with his pinky finger. In his seventies, his hair had once been black, but was now frosty white. His body had once been muscled, but now sagged. I recognized him right away.

"Mr. Bornado."

"Eh?" He looked up, sternly at first, then a gleeful smile came over his face. "Little Jack. Well, I'll be damned." Even as old as he was, the man still had a ruddy complexion as if he spent every spare hour out under the sun. Several of his teeth were missing now, creating holes in his smile.

"Hey, Mr. Bornado."

Obviously happy to see me, he cackled and twisted his head to the side. He probed my face with his eyes. "How are you, boy?"

"I'm good, sir. As good as can be expected." I gave him a perfunctory smile.

He scrunched up his face in regret. "That's a terrible business with your daddy." He shook his head from side to side and made a *tsking* sound. "But truth be told, Big Jack was one pissed off son of a bitch."

I nodded calmly, looking down at the shrunken man in front of me. His skin was discolored along his hands, forehead and nose, mottled with patches of mauve or red. Though his body had lost its bullish mass, his eyes still bulged in their sockets with infernal vigor.

"No, I mean it...you might not see this 'cause he was your daddy and you loved him, but I mean he was just always mad as hell. I never understood it." His voice was twice as loud as necessary and it boomed off the walls. "Every single time I tried to stop your daddy to talk, he acted like I was a horse thief or something."

I smiled, caught between amusement and loathing. "Dad had problems." *Most likely, one of those problems was that he didn't enjoy the thought of your hairy ass pounding the fuck out of his wife.*

"...just always pissed off, even out at the plant. Some of the boys just didn't even wanna work with him." Tilting his head down for emphasis, he balled his fist and held up a crooked, knotted finger, poking me in the chest to punctuate his words.

BIG JACK is DEAD

My jaws locked together when he touched me. *An urge came over me, to grab his arm and yank until the gristle popped in his shoulder. I saw myself biting down on the claw of his finger, crunching and slicing through the first knuckle with my teeth, taking him by the throat and throwing him through the window. I imagined him lying in the gravel and leaves just outside the window, covered in his own blood, shards of glass rising from his body and trembling with his breath like the fins and plates of some decrepit dinosaur in its death throes.*

"Hey!" The old man looked up, grinning maniacally. "I saw your momma out there." He looked up into at my face with wide-eyed excitement. Pinching up his mouth, he squinted as if in pain. "Ooh...she looks rough, don't she?"

I actually laughed out loud. "Yes, sir, I believe she does. She looks rough." *Then again, so do you.* Running my tongue over my teeth, I wondered how much longer Mr. Bornado would walk the world. How many years, or months, until he fell and broke a hip, or forgot where he was one too many times.

"Yeah," he said. "She looks real rough."

"Well, it's good to see you, Mr. Bornado, but I need to go get ready."

"Aw, yeah, aw, yeah. I'll see ya out there." He turned and angled around me, moving down the sunlit hall, his gait mechanical, broken.

Listening to him shuffle away, I stared out the window into the courtyard. When he was gone, I headed toward the funeral hall to take my place.

The off-kilter quality of the day continued; everyone was in the right place, more or less wearing the right clothes for the occasion, but no one was quite sure how to act; nothing felt right. Everyone attending Big Jack's funeral seemed bewildered. There was confusion in the air and latent tension layered over it. Is it possible to miss someone like him? Does anyone really feel sad about this?

I chose to sit at the far end of the first pew, closest to the wall and farthest from the center aisle, with Brodie at my left. Mincy and Ramona sat further down. They rarely spoke, but occasionally my stepmother directed my mother in some small way...sliding her down the pew a few inches, telling her to pick up her hymnal or tuck her purse back further under the seat. Ramona did these things slowly, but without question. Mincy watched her with what seemed like concern, which surprised me.

BIG JACK is DEAD

The only light in the chamber filtered in from eight stained glass windows that were vaguely religious, but technically non-denominational. An organ player sat at the front of the room, a rail thin woman wearing enormous glasses. She barely moved as her hands crawled deliberately over the keys. Between each song, she paused for thirty seconds then nodded to herself twice as she launched into the next piece.

Handling all the arrangements with efficiency, Mincy had reserved the facility and hired both the preacher and the organ player. My stepmother hadn't been married to Dad for many years, but she was undoubtedly the right person to manage the affair of his funeral. The preacher she enlisted had never met my father, but Big Jack was not known to keep the company of preachers, or to keep the company of any other men save co-workers from the plant or the occasional deer hunter he met out on a lease.

The preacher waited off to the side, ready to begin. He was stout, with red hair and pink skin. Shifting in his seat, he adjusted his portly frame, applying lip balm so often that I wanted to get up and take the small tube away from him.

The door opened, filling the entryway with overpowering sunlight. Ricky was one of my father's oldest hunting buddies. Swaying on his feet, he swung the door wide and held it back for several others, including Jenny. As she passed, he stared hypnotically at her ass cheeks as they shifted from side to side beneath the shimmer of her skirt. Once everyone was inside, he pulled the heavy door, slamming it too hard then fumbling with the handle until he got it closed and the last sliver of light was eclipsed.

Jenny stood tentatively in the light shining through the stained glass windows. The closest window depicted a woman in amethyst and teal standing on the bank of a river. In the watery light, Jenny looked like a mermaid. Comfort came over me; she was at least a part of my history that I'd chosen. I stood up, facing her and straightening my jacket. The people in the pews around me looked up, unsure of what I was doing. Some of them craned their heads and followed my gaze. When Jenny noticed, I smiled and gestured for her to join me.

When she got close, she said, "Are you sure?" Leaning toward me, she mouthed the words, worried about breaking decorum by sitting with the family. The notion that the people around me had the right to insist on enforcing rigid social laws made me want to smash the windows. I took her hand and waited for my family to scoot down, which took a while as Mincy gently scolded Ramona into action. My mother rose stiffly while everyone waited to take their new positions. As Jenny settled in next to me, I could feel her warmth through the thin material of my suit.

Ricky spotted Kohen and made his way to the back aisle, weaving and wobbling as he negotiated his way past the others seated at the rear of the chamber. He looked roughly the same, unchanged by time. He was still cobby-shouldered with very little body fat and the stiff bearing of the men who worked heavy labor jobs out at the plant. I envisioned him sitting in the truck before coming into the funeral home, draining a beer for nerve and crushing the can, the same way he'd worked up his courage the first time he'd humped some pimply rodeo queen at seventeen. He wore cream-colored cowboy boots, jeans and a Western shirt under a jacket with coattails that reached his knees. His blond hair was still thick and curly, though it contained more gray now. His clothing and hair combined to give him the appearance of some fairy tale dwarf, just emerged from the forest, ready to pose riddles to the townsfolk in exchange for a captured infant. Startling both Brodie and Jenny, I laughed as I watched Ricky drop down onto the seat next to Kohen.

As the funeral started, the red-headed preacher spoke with great reverence for a man he had never known, painting a noble portrait of my ridiculous father. "The Bible says, the father of the righteous shall greatly rejoice, for he that begets a wise child shall have joy in him. And we all know that the late Jack Hickman was the kind of righteous and wise man who in turn brought into this world righteous and wise sons, for the child is in the making of the father, always and forever, Amen."

The hypocrisy was offensive, another onslaught. I slitted my eyes and listened as the stubby preacher stood behind the pulpit and talked about my father's "community service" and lifelong membership in the Christian Rifle Association. Looking at the ceiling, I took in a big breath, trying to let go of my tension.

Each time I remembered why we were gathered, I felt a small shock. My eyes lit upon my father's calm face and my senses reeled, the church shifted. His death and this ritual did not fit into my view of the world.

The preacher raised his eyes to the ceiling. "He is with the angels now."

I saw my father standing in the company of angels, twisting his head to look up at them, his eyes wild and red-rimmed. They were tall and beautiful, with infinite understanding and compassion. My father, stunted and filthy. I tore into them, firing a handgun into their beautiful faces at point blank range. They shrieked and wailed as I poured gasoline over their feathered wings.

Several women were crying now. My mother continued her stunned oozing while my stepmother made a much bigger show of it, sobbing into a lace handkerchief. Midway back, a plump woman with blond and gray hair also cried. Her hair matched Ricky's almost perfectly and I recognized her as Shirley, the doughnut waitress. Over the years, I'd seen her around my father enough to suspect that they'd carried on a long-running affair.

At the high point of the ceremony, the preacher opened a songbook. "Now we'll all sing *Always Watches Over Me*," he said. "I'm told this was Jack Hickman's favorite hymn… the one he loved most as a boy and as a man."

I nearly burst out laughing at the notion that my father had a favorite hymn or any other favorite thing about church, but I opened the songbook, holding half of it while Jenny and I sang along.

Out in the shadows, there I've seen Him,
The one who shed His blood for me;
He'll come down on wings against the Seraphim,
The one I know is watching me.

We all rose when it was over. Starting with the front row, everyone filed past the casket. The crowd moved slowly, sharing the same discomfort as they drew near. The music swelled as the organ player began the final song of the service. In the casket, Big Jack lay perfectly still, his face childlike. He was lit dramatically, like a stuffed creature in a taxidermy case.

One hand came to my mouth unconsciously as I approached the coffin. To my surprise, I choked, making no sound, but convulsively gasping for air. Jenny grabbed my hand as I teetered backward, on the edge of collapse. She squeezed and pulled me along. Thank you.

At my back, I heard my mother's voice. "Oh...there ain't no bag on his face or nothing."

"Ramona," Mincy squawked, "Don't say that."

The line continued making progress toward the back of the room then Jenny and I were away. Suddenly, it was over and we were outside, under a carport. We walked to my rental car, still holding hands. Others milled by the back doors, smoking. Some of them stood in the parking lot, trying to work out carpooling arrangements for the funeral procession. Next to the car, I pulled Jenny against me, holding her to my body tightly. She reached up with one hand and took the back of my head, burying it against her neck.

"Baby," she said.

Inside the Lexus, I told her, "I'm glad you were here."

When everyone else was ready, the hearse moved into place and flashed its lights. Driving our mother, Brodie backed out and fell into place. I waited for a minute then slid into the next spot. Mincy and her latest husband were in the next car, with him behind the wheel. I could see her sobbing into her hands. Eventually, the entire line of cars and trucks rolled out onto the road next to the funeral home and we began the twenty-minute drive to the cemetery.

At the first major traffic light, I leaned over and pulled Jenny closer. I kissed her, softly at first then aggressively. She responded, hesitating only when I pressed her hand into my lap.

"Now?" There was surprise on her face and her accent twanged, giving the word multiple syllables.

"I swear I'm losing my mind," I said.

Jenny turned her head slightly, looking into the street.

"No one will see you. The windows are dark."

Her eyes showed concern, but she began kneading my erection through the black cloth. Working together, we got the zipper down. Jenny looked around once more then leaned into my shoulder. Hooking the band of my underwear with her thumb, she stretched them out of the way. I released my belt buckle, giving her more room.

HARVEY SMITH

As I accelerated through an intersection, Jenny lowered herself down and I cried out in ecstasy at the contact with her mouth.

Chapter 15

1980

Autumn came limping into Lowfield, a half-hearted change from the heat and humidity characterizing most of the year...roach weather, as Big Jack liked to call it because of the long, black insects that crawled or flew across the town at night during the warm months. Nothing on the Gulf Coast resembled what people elsewhere would call *fall*; autumn meant that jaundice crept into the leaves, clamminess into the air, and a chilly drizzle fell every day.

When Jack found the car, Ramona and his brother were waiting. Other kids swarmed the area, moving along the sidewalk in front of the school, armed with backpacks and lunch boxes, crying out like birds.

"I got the front," Brodie said.

Jack ignored him and slid behind his mother's seat, into the back. He was thirteen and attended the only middle school in Lowfield. Brodie, only eight, went to one of the elementary schools dotting the town.

Ramona slipped it into gear and joined the line of vehicles leaving the parking lot. Big Jack had finally gotten her a car, a ten-year-old Honda hatchback that was eaten down to the frame with rust. It coughed and backfired as she pulled away.

Halfway home, she turned into Sonny's Gas and Bait for cigarettes, buying her brand and her husband's. Before returning, she made a call from the pay phone on the sidewalk outside the store while the boys waited in the car. Brodie sang and kicked the dash, watching her. Tuning him out, Jack watched black-feathered grackles outside the window, hunting through the grass for bugs.

Five minutes later, Ramona turned onto the block where they lived. As it often did, the car died, but they were close enough to the house that she just coasted to the curb and put it into park. Brodie wrestled with the door and threw it open. The bottom edge scraped the curb, screeching as he jumped out onto the sidewalk. He ran toward the porch with a pile of drawings in one hand. Carrying his books, Jack followed. Ramona trailed behind, struggling to rip a pack of cigarettes from the carton.

A strange suitcase sat on the living room coffee table. There were letters across the side that said Myerson and Sons, a brand of door-to-door cosmetics peddled by agents roaming the town. As Ramona and the boys stood looking at the makeup case, Big Jack and Mincy emerged from the hallway.

Big Jack rounded the corner with his mouth agape. "What are y'all doing home?"

"The boys just got off school," Ramona said. She smiled at Mincy, who stood blinking. "Looks like you just about missed me again. You always come by when I'm out doing somethin'."

"I wanted to show you our fall collection," Mincy said.

"Oh...well let me get settled and we can look at it." She dropped her purse and cigarettes on the coffee table next to the makeup case. "Though you know he won't let me spend any money on stuff like this." Gesturing at Big Jack, she curled her lips into something between jovial and sneering. She paused. "What was y'all doing in there?"

Big Jack pointed back to the bedroom. "I was just showing her that sink I fixed last week."

"Oh," Ramona said.

The boys went into the kitchen, hunting food. Brodie watched while Jack piled sandwich materials on the counter. He made several bologna and cheese sandwiches, putting everything in place except the meat. Hefting a cast iron skillet onto the stove, he added oil and started the burner. Five pieces of lunchmeat sat on the counter top in a line. Starting in the center of each round slice, Jack cut outward to the edges so the meat wouldn't puff up like a basketball when it cooked. He fried the lunchmeat, mashing it flat with a spatula. Once the bologna was black, he scooped up each slice and dropped it onto the mayonnaise-covered bread, melting the American cheese underneath. On side-by-side paper towels, he divided the sandwiches. Then the two boys sat down at the dinner table and started eating.

There was an argument underway in the living room. This was a common occurrence, but usually their parents only fought when no one was visiting. Suddenly they were screaming so loudly that it gave Jack a chill. Even Mincy was involved.

"You oughta go to your room and play," Jack said to Brodie calmly.

His little brother nodded with a mouthful of food, wrapping up the remainder of his sandwiches. The paper towel was so greasy now that it was translucent. He tip-toed down the hall toward his bedroom, balancing the bundle in one hand.

Jack got up to follow him after a minute, grabbing his own food and heading for the back of the house. As he passed his parents' bedroom, he noticed something strange. Like a burglary scene in a cop show, half the dresser drawers were open, sticking out haphazardly, strewn with shirts and underwear. The closet door was open and the light was on, a dim bulb hanging nakedly from a cord. Something stood out as wrong, but Jack couldn't identify it. Holding his last sandwich, he took a furtive step into the bedroom and looked around.

All of his mother's clothes were missing from the closet and dresser. Her cheap shoes were gone from the rack on the backside of the door. Her dresses and pants were no longer hanging along the back wall of the closet. Instead, Jack was confronted with a blank wall and a few naked hangers. The bed was unmade, a mess of ripped quilts, ancient pillows and threadbare sheets. The food in Jack's mouth went cold and his stomach turned.

The living room door slammed.

"Boy, get in here," Big Jack yelled.

Jack crept into the hall just as Brodie stepped into the doorway of his bedroom. Brodie looked up at his older brother, unsure.

"You stay in your room," Jack whispered. He handed Brodie his last sandwich and turned around. Brodie bit into the sandwich, watching Jack disappear down the hall.

Big Jack was sitting in his recliner and Mincy was sitting on the couch in front of her makeup case.

Taking a drag on his cigarette, Big Jack cocked an eyebrow. "Boy, I got some bad news."

Jack studied his father's face, dreading his next words. Something distracted him and he looked through the living room window. Ramona stood on the porch. She stared at the front door, mouth wide.

Jack winced. "Why is Mom outside?" he asked, watching her. She seemed unable to move.

"Goddammit," Big Jack said. He hopped up from the recliner and yanked the door back. He stepped into the opening, blocking Ramona when she tried to enter. "I told you...your shit is at your momma's and you can have that car." He waited a minute, but Ramona did not speak. "Goddammit, woman...you can't stay here no more. You got to go. If you don't, I'm gonna call the law..."

Ramona didn't move. Her mouth still hung open.

"What's going on?" Jack asked.

Big Jack whirled and pointed a calloused finger at his son. "You shut the fuck up if you know what's good for you."

Jack went silent, taking on a dead expression.

Big Jack turned back to Ramona. "Now get the fuck out. Get off my property. Take your car and go to your momma's. Every bit of your shit is there." He looked over his shoulder at Mincy, on the couch. Her face was flush and she gripped the hem of her skirt, working the fabric with her plump fingers.

Leaning out through the doorframe, closer to Ramona, Big Jack hissed at her in a voice Jack had never heard before. "You got about five fucking seconds to walk your ass down to that car and get the fuck out of here before I do something you ain't gonna like."

Mincy got up as fast as she could, causing the couch to undulate and the springs to groan. She crossed the floor and stood next to Big Jack. "You've got to go, Ramona. If he calls the law, you'll be going to prison. You've just got to go." She reached out with one finger and poked the other woman roughly in the stomach. "You can't do that around them boys... If the police hear one word of it, you'll spend the rest of your life behind bars and I promise you won't like that." She pursed her lips as she finished speaking.

Big Jack leaned further forward. "Git. The fuck. Out."

Ramona's face lost all color. She turned and fled down the walk. Opening the door to the Honda, she slipped behind the wheel and sat looking forward, motionless except for quick glances back at the front door.

When she drove away, Big Jack closed the front door. Mincy put one hand on his shoulder and rubbed it.

"That was hard," she said. "I know it was hard, but you had to do it for these boys." She indicated Jack with an open palm. He stood near the coffee table, a stunned look on his face.

"Yeah, I know," Big Jack said. The vein in the center of his forehead was so swollen that it looked like it was going to rupture. He looked at Mincy then his son. "Boy, I hate to tell you this...I know it's just terrible. But your momma was smokin' marijuana." He scrutinized Jack, waiting for his words to sink in. "And that ain't right around you and your little brother." He slowed down, trying to explain. "Niggers use drugs. Drugs ain't good." He shook his head in time with the last three words.

Mincy spoke up from beside him. "Your father told her that he was going to call the police if she didn't leave. You can't say anything to little Brodie, but the social services would have taken you boys away from your daddy and put you into a foster home." Her eyes rolled up toward the ceiling again, exclusively white. "...maybe even separate foster homes."

Jack stood perfectly still, watching her.

Seeing that he was unconvinced, she continued. "You're thirteen, so you're old enough to know about this, but Brodie isn't...you can't tell him about any of these matters."

Jack turned to his father. "You came home early to pack up her clothes and stuff?"

"I had to, boy!" Big Jack was incensed by the question. "She'd woulda fought tooth and nail if I hadn't. I didn't want to have to call Johnny Poe-leece on her ass." He gazed at his son for a minute, somewhat lost. "You don't want your momma in jail, do you?"

"No." Jack spoke quietly, but he wanted to scream, wanted to ask more questions, but he knew that his father would not provide the answers. Already pushing his luck to the limit, he felt growing caution. His father's patience was unpredictably thin. "What's gonna happen?" Jack asked.

Big Jack looked at Mincy first then his son. "Well...it'll be just us men for a while. We'll be alright." He grinned at Jack. "Hell, boy...might even be fun around here."

A couple of weeks after Ramona moved out, Jack heard his father's truck pull into the driveway at roughly the same time it always did. His stomach rumbled to life as the engine died. Big Jack brought fast food home each night instead of cooking. Usually, it was fried chicken, sometimes burgers.

Jack noticed something different this time, but he wasn't sure what it was. Only when he heard voices raised in conversation and laughter did he realize that two truck doors had slammed instead of one. Resting his paperback on the carpet and sitting up from the couch, he watched his father and Mincy unloading luggage from the bed of the truck. As Big Jack hauled her suitcases up to the front door, she followed with an excited, breathless expression.

Big Jack entered through the front door and piled everything on the carpet by his recliner. "Phew," he said. "Goddamn, woman."

Mincy giggled, standing on the doorstep. She looked at Big Jack expectantly. He searched her face before realizing what she wanted.

"Oh…shit," he said. "Hang on." He walked over to the doorway and made an effort to lift her up.

Jack watched from the couch, curious and wary.

His father looped his arms under Mincy's enormous ass and heaved her a few inches off the ground, gasping as he did. They managed to stagger forward by a foot or two, nearly toppling before Big Jack released her just inside the doorway. When he stood up, his face was red. Grunting, he put a hand on the small of his back. Mincy smiled delicately, smoothing her flower-printed skirt.

Big Jack noticed his son. "Hey, boy. Where's your brother?

"In his bedroom, I think."

"Brodie!" Big Jack bellowed. "Brodie, get in here."

A few seconds later, the younger boy peeked around the corner from the hallway. He crossed the living room and inched backward onto the couch beside Jack.

"Boys," Big Jack said, "Mincy and me got something to tell you. Good news."

"Is Momma coming home?" Brodie asked.

Mincy stood next to Big Jack, looking down at the boy with heavily-lidded eyes. "No, Brodie, your mother can't come home. If she does, she'll get in trouble with the law because she is a dope user."

Brodie looked confused. He looked from Mincy's face to his father's.

"What we gotta tell you is this," Big Jack said. He took in a deep breath. "Mincy'll be moving into the house with us." He tried to smile at his sons. "That'll be good, huh?"

Fear settled over Brodie's face as he began to whine. "You said Momma was coming back."

Big Jack lunged toward the eight year old, "Your momma fucks niggers now, boy. She ain't never comin' back."

Brodie gazed up at his father.

Jack tensed for his brother's cries, bracing himself for the outpour that accompanied such interactions with their father, but this time Brodie was silent.

Chapter 16

1999

At the cemetery, we stood under an awning erected over the site. Big Jack's casket was suspended over his grave, held in place by the straps that would lower him into the ground. A wreath of flowers sat on top of the coffin.

I studied the darkness of the grave through a gap between the bottom of the coffin and the neat edge of the earth. A specialized machine had extracted a perfect geometric cavity from the ground. The machine was mounted to the back of a tractor parked nearby, thick slices of mud stuck to its blades. Indoor-outdoor carpet was spread over the area to protect our dress shoes from the fresh mud. The wind blew through the massive pecan trees in the old graveyard, sending the occasional branch or husked pecan down into the grass below.

I looked at the coffin and trembled. *My father is in that dark space. He will never come out.* I felt the world changing again in some fundamental way.

The ceremony was short. The preacher read a passage from the Bible and led us in prayer. About half the people from the funeral were there to see Big Jack settle into his final resting place. They began to disperse when the preacher finished his last rites. Watching them head off to their cars and trucks, I knew I would never see most of them again. I stood for a long time with Jenny, Mincy, Ramona and Brodie.

Two black men who worked for the cemetery hovered nearby, waiting to lower the casket down into the earth. One of them asked, "Y'all want us to wait some more?" His expression was neutral, just a man at work, asking a question about the job and wanting to get out of the wind. "We can come back…"

Everyone turned to face me. "No," I said. "Go ahead and do it."

"You don't wanna watch this," Brodie said.

Something about his earnestness made me want to hit him. It smacked of a folksy simplicity that he lacked. *After all the shit he showed us when he was alive? And by the way you looked at the goddamn police photos of the suicide.* I almost said it aloud, but held my tongue, too exhausted to fight.

"Yes, I do. I'll stay. Everyone else can leave…I don't care." I released Jenny's hand and leaned over to kiss her cheek. "Thank you," I whispered.

HARVEY SMITH

"Well, we're gonna go," Mincy said. She came over and hugged Brodie, then me, something I found touching. Some of my tension eased. Stepping back, she took my mother's upper arm and led her away. Ramona had a strange smile on her face and held one hand curled like a talon between her sagging breasts. Mincy made eye contact with me a last time and smiled. Jenny reached up to touch my shoulder briefly then followed the other women.

Once they were gone, I turned to one of the cemetery workers and nodded. He ambled over to the lift and it rattled to life, coughing out blue-white smoke and the cloying smell of diesel. It spooled out the canvas straps supporting the coffin, lowering it into the grave.

Unsure of what to do, I reached down and took up a clod of dirt lying on the indoor-outdoor carpet. When the top of the casket dropped below the surface of the ground, I released the dirt and it fell with a thump onto the metallic surface. Brodie watched me then did the same.

Chapter 17

1980

On a winter evening in Lowfield, Big Jack called his sons out into the front yard. They stood in their coats with the hoods up, every breath a puff of white air. Jack stood next to Brodie, watching their father mumble to himself and move about the yard.

"Hard fucking freeze comin' tonight." Throwing it over one shoulder, he pulled a garden hose further into the center of the yard. "S'posed to get down to fifteen goddamn degrees." From the back pocket of his jeans, he drew out a fan-shaped sprinkler head and attached it to a second garden hose. Both hoses snaked off to the side of the house where they connected to the spigot. Using tent stakes and old wire from his shop in the garage, he positioned the hoses so that they pointed up toward the tall Chinaberry tree in the front yard. During the warmer months, the boys climbed in the branches of the tree and picked the hard berries to throw at one another.

"Dad, whatcha doing?" Brodie asked.

Bent at the waist, Big Jack turned toward them and smiled with a kind of secretive glee. "You watch, boy." He continued to make adjustments, forcing a tent stake deeper into the cold ground and tightening a wire.

"Okay, go turn it on," he said to Jack.

Moving into the cold shadow between the two houses, Jack treaded along stiffly in his coat, wary of dog shit. Standing close to the foundation of the house, he could feel the cold coming off the concrete. As he cranked the valve to maximum, the hose shifted under the pressure and a spray of mist emerged around the spigot where the hose was imperfectly threaded.

As he reached the corner of the house, he slowed because he could hear his father cursing.

"Now goddammit, boy. Did I ask you to turn it on all the way?"

Jack stopped, studying his father. "I thought you wanted it on," he said.

Brodie looked back and forth between the two of them.

A menacing, disgusted expression crossed Big Jack's face. "I did want it on. Just not all the fuckin' way. You better use your goddamn head." He pointed at his head with two fingers, jabbing himself in the temple. "Turn it on halfway."

Jack stared, demeanor sullen, but his father didn't seem to notice. Returning to the side of the house, Jack's face was red, his jaw clenched. He kicked at the dried body of a toad, hit by the lawnmower weeks before and stripped by fire ants. Balling his fists, he beat them four times against his thighs. The light was falling fast and the air was colder. Through the nearly naked branches of a bush, he could see an abandoned bird nest. Letting out a deep sigh, he cut the flow of water by roughly half before returning to the front yard, where the sprinkler sent a flat arc up into the branches of the Chinaberry tree.

The air was full of water vapor and the chilly weather was suddenly more miserable. Huddling in his coat, Jack took up his position next to Brodie. Their father joined them and lit up a cigarette. They all stood together and watched the deluge for a minute or two.

Big Jack's mood shifted entirely. Working his mouth around the cigarette, he chuckled to himself. "You just wait. This shit is gonna be pretty slick in the morning."

A car coming down the street slowed as it passed the house, the driver twisting to gawk at the tree and the sprinklers, mouth open. Jack could barely discern the pale face of another passenger, leaning forward in curiosity. Big Jack scowled at them and the car sped up, cherry taillights shrinking in the distance. He turned to go inside and the boys followed him.

That night a hard freeze hit Lowfield, as predicted. The cold weather burst pipes and killed off houseplants across town. The next morning, everything was covered in a layer of ice. The sidewalks and roads were slick and treacherous.

As Jack awoke, he could hear his father bellowing in the living room. At first the words made no sense, coming from far away. He blinked as he woke up, arching his spine and stretching his arms overhead until they made contact with the cool, white wall. As always, he'd thrashed in his sleep, tangling the sheets and the blanket. Exposed, the skin on his chest was chill to the touch.

He groaned and rolled over onto his stomach, grinding his erection into the mattress. Even at thirteen, he still sometimes peed in the bed, which confused and mortified him, but this morning his sheets were dry. Closing his eyes, he let waves of pleasure wash over him as he pressed himself down into the bed, humping slowly a few times. He considered slipping into the bathroom to masturbate before breakfast, but his father called out again.

"Boys, come see!" Big Jack cackled and said something inaudible. When only silence returned from their bedrooms, he yelled, "Goddamn it. Get up, you little fuckers!"

Jack rolled out of bed and landed on his bare feet. Brodie bumped the wall in the next bedroom as he jolted awake.

Jack's room was very neat, almost empty. He crossed the floor and opened a drawer, pulling out a pair of sweatpants and tugging them on. Struggling with the drawstring, he hoped the sweats would hide his erection. When he came into the living room, he was still unsteady from sleep.

"Hurry the fuck up," his father said.

Mincy entered just ahead of Jack, wearing a silky robe that revealed much of her cleavage and only covered the rest of her body down to the mid-thigh. Her ass was several times larger than Jack's head and each of her thick legs was deeply dimpled. She moved up next to Big Jack, looping an arm around his waist and cupping the blade of his hip bone through his jeans, which he'd donned upon leaping from bed. She stood roughly the height of her husband and craned her neck to see out into the yard.

Big Jack pointed out through the front window. "Look at that shit. It worked!"

"Oh my god," Mincy said.

Big Jack looked at her sharply, surprised by her reaction. Staring at her briefly, his mouth drooped and his eyes showed concern, but the expression changed to pride as he realized that she was impressed.

Jack walked over next to them, slipping between the recliner and an end table, moving up against the window.

Mincy's flesh shifted beneath the robe, causing him to shudder with lust.

Out in the yard, the Chinaberry tree was completely encased in ice.

Staring out the window, his father spoke with reverence. "Looks like goddamn Disneyland, don't it?"

Big Jack's handiwork dominated the front yard. The area was so radically changed that Jack's breath caught in his throat. Ice encrusted the Chinaberry tree to its full height, extending out along all its branches. The spray from the water hoses had cascaded down around it for ten feet in all directions, freezing drop upon drop through the night until the tree itself was lost. It resembled a raging fountain, frozen in mid-torrent. All around the yard, the grass was stiff and ghostly.

While there was no snow, the entire block was frosted over, the weather leeching much of the color from the world. Everything was gray or white and the sky overhead was a monochrome void. Just over the houses across the street, the first pale sunlight was evident. Everything was more still than usual.

Brodie trundled up behind them and stood quiet. Eyes wide, he was stunned with excitement.

"That's just so pretty," Mincy said in disbelief. She turned and tilted her head, pecking Big Jack on the cheek. "We've just never had anything so pretty."

They all stood at the window. Jack could feel the cold reaching his skin through the glass, but the view was mesmerizing.

"Let's go outside and look at it up close," Big Jack said. When he snapped his head toward his sons they both jumped from the sudden motion. "Don't fucking touch it," he said. The vein on his forehead puffed up in an instant and looked like it was going to pop. After holding them in his gaze, he made his way into the kitchen to refill his coffee cup. The others moved through the house to put on warmer clothes.

At the coat rack by the front door, Jack slid into his puffer jacket, zipping it up over his bare chest. His erection had melted away, forgotten at the sight of the ice tree. He ran back to his room for some sneakers and put them on without socks. Jack and his father made it outside first while Mincy was helping Brodie get dressed in his room.

Among the houses on the block, their yard was now utterly unique.

The early rays of the sun hit parts of the tree and the ice gleamed at the far tips of the branches. Dawn cast a faint, skeletal shadow against the side of the house. From the yard, the thing standing before them loomed even larger and more grandiose, with pockets and crevices all through the branches and flowing arms of ice. As the air gusted up, it whistled or moaned through the tree. Jack could barely make out a hummingbird feeder frozen a couple of feet deep within the folds of ice.

"Ain't this somethin'?" Big Jack asked. His eyes bulged in wonder. "It's bigger'n Henry's whole tool shed."

Jack gazed up at the tree, awed. "It's really great, Dad."

After a few minutes, Mincy and Brodie joined them on the sidewalk next to the crunchy grass. Brodie nearly slipped once, teetering toward the curb, but Big Jack deftly reached out and righted him by the top of his head.

They all stared at the tree, occasionally changing positions to get a different vantage point, walking carefully along the icy sidewalk.

"What do we do with it?" Brodie asked.

Big Jack looked incredulous, bordering on dismayed. "What the fuck you mean, boy? We look at it. That's all."

Brodie looked down at the white grass. "Oh."

"Mmm," Mincy said. "You know what we should do to celebrate this?"

Big Jack smiled at her. "Yeah, what's that?"

"We should go down to the Pancake Palace for breakfast," she said. There was a wide grin on her face. Big Jack opened his mouth to say something, but Mincy cut him off, leaving him agape. "Now, baby...you did real good and we should celebrate. I'm proud of you." She threw her meaty arms around his neck and pressed her body against him.

Before anyone else could speak, she shooed the boys into the house. They got dressed and Big Jack drove them to breakfast.

Chapter 18

1999

Mincy handled everything before I flew home for the funeral, renting a storage space and coordinating with Big Jack's landlord. The man was extremely upset that one of his tenants had killed himself on the property, and insisted that everything be moved out as soon as the police investigation was complete. There was a new tenant waiting. The bank impounded Big Jack's truck to cover his streak of hot checks, so the storage unit contained all that was left in the world of my father.

It was located in a strip mall next to Doyle's Patty Kitchen, a burger place. Crossing the parking lot, all I could smell was the grease trap behind the buildings.

Inside the storage facility, the lobby was all white... counters, walls, floor and ceiling. Two sets of automatic glass doors kept the air chilled and the entire place hummed, every surface vibrating slightly to the touch. Beyond the lobby, a network of hallways led to identical doors, where a number was inscribed on each door in black lettering. The place reminded me of the stylized hotel in Hamburg, a high-tech mausoleum as envisioned by Bauhaus. The orderliness was somehow at odds with the hamburger place and drive through liquor store nearby.

Taking the key from the man behind the desk, I walked down one of the long white aisles lined with modular storage units. Earlier, I'd changed out of my suit and back to my jeans.

At door #66, I checked the number against the key ring. Everything on all sides was white. The place continued to hum so pervasively that even the air trembled. I turned the key and pulled the door aside. Several fluorescent lights came on automatically, running the length of the space. It was four feet wide and six feet deep. The ceiling was just high enough so that I didn't have to duck.

The ruddy odor of blood hit me as I stepped inside, followed by the stench of soiled laundry. I squinted my eyes, reeling. Several plastic bags sat against the back wall of the room. Everything from the rental house had been stuffed into trash bags. I wondered who collected his things and why they chose trash bags.

There was something stunning about the bags. This was the cumulative results of Dad's life, aside from a landscape of emotional scar tissue. Somewhere there were records of his various worldly transactions; hot checks, bankruptcies, occasional run-ins with the law, a high school transcript and his employment history. But here in this small cell were the only things he left behind. It seemed pathetic that it could all be contained in six or eight trash bags.

I walked over and sank down to the floor, holding my breath against the smell. The tiles of the floor hummed beneath me, the soulless fluorescent lights flickered above. Teasing apart the loose knot, I began going through the first of the black bags. Mostly they contained my father's unwashed clothes. Greasy jeans, scorched welding shirts, socks and underwear...the basis for ninety percent of his wardrobe. There were candy bar wrappers everywhere, scattered throughout the clothing like random bits of newspaper in a bird's nest. Too-sweet chocolate wafted over me as I scooped them up by the handfuls and wadded them tight. I started a waste pile just outside the door.

Sifting through the clothing, touching the last things my father had worn, made me wish I could talk to him, or just sit with him while he drank coffee and smoked. Those were the calmest, sanest moments I could remember.

Alternately, my lip curled in disgust when I grabbed something crusty and stiff. I wanted to scream at him for putting me through this shit, the shock of his self-destruction. As if growing up with him wasn't enough, there was the funeral, and now the touch of his grimy belongings and the smell of his spilled blood.

But he was gone. His death robbed me of the chance to tear into him, leaving me with impossible nostalgia and impossible fury all in the same intake of breath.

Carefully, I rifled each item of clothing. When handling a pair of jeans, no matter how tattered, I turned all the pockets inside out. I tore shirts to pieces, opening flaps and stripping the pockets down. At one point, I found myself looking for hidden compartments sewn into the fabric, shredding a camouflage puffer vest in my hands, methodically taking it apart at the seams. It felt crazy, but I finished ripping it up anyway. The clothes went into the garbage pile with the food wrappers.

There were a dozen magazines and a few paperbacks, dedicated to porn or hunting. The only hard bound book was new, a manual on raising and training bird dogs. I flipped through all of them, page by page. The naked women made me shudder with discomfort, imaging Dad staring at them in a lusty daze. On the bottom of the stack, there was an envelope stuffed with receipts and small scraps of paper that I read before crumpling and discarding. The garbage pile grew.

Twisting the cap off his thermos, I looked inside, sniffing and reeling at the rank odor of coffee that had spoiled a week ago. As I unscrewed the lid, I fantasized about a rolled note sliding out into my lap...some letter that would provide me with clues about the devils that drove him, or some final sentiment.

After looking over every bit of my father's belongings, my hands were filthy with unnameable grime, part industrial, part animal. My senses were saturated, the odors so dulled that I barely noticed them. Gathering the trash pile, I stuffed it all into a few empty bags and carried them to a dumpster in the corner of the parking lot.

When I returned to the storage room, I took stock of what remained, pushing or tossing everything into the center of the floor...some of my father's tools, a heavily-shielded welding mask, a photo album, and his wallet. Everything else was gone, ready to be broken down by incineration or rot, including the man himself.

The toolbox was mostly full of odd screwdrivers and wrenches. A layer of screws and washers lined the bottom like coins in a sunken chest. The tools were mismatched, coming from four or five different tool sets. I suspected that my father's primary tools, the ones he used at work, had been stolen by someone along the way between the rental house and the storage unit. Likewise, his guns were nowhere to be seen. A pawnshop somewhere in the county probably owned them now. Aside from the tools, the battered toolbox contained two tape measures, an old pencil, a few oily rags, and a roll of pipefitter's tape. I lifted and inspected each item before replacing it.

My father's welding mask looked up at me from the floor, the black glass inscrutable. I ran my fingers over the cool surface of the visor, remembering a moment from twenty-five years earlier. It came to me vividly...I must have been around five, accompanying my mother on a rare trip into the plant where my father worked. In her sister's battered car, Ramona drove us off the highway and up to the chain link checkpoint. Holding a paper cup in one hand, an ancient man came out of the small shack, badly bowlegged. He approached the window to check my mother's identification card, working his lower jaw as he studied it. He spat tobacco juice into the cup and allowed us to pass.

I was fascinated with the high fence, with the curling barbed wire running along the uppermost edge, and the dense skyline of smokestacks, towers and industrial structures beyond the entry gate. At the same time, the place was foreboding, dead and inorganic, an environment hostile to life. The air stank and burned my nose.

We finally located my father's shop and parked. Ramona led me by the hand to where my father was welding. Standing back twenty feet, she chatted and laughed with another man as we waited.

I pointed to Dad and said something, but no one heard me. He was kneeling next to a framework of pipe that looked like the hollow, black bones of some monster. There were massive leather gloves protecting his hands and his welding mask fully encased the top of his head, his face and throat. A billed cap, turned around, was visible on the back of his head, the bill guarding the nape of his neck from sparks and slag. The welding machine was deafening. My father's shadow was cast starkly behind him on the scorched concrete. His back was soaked with sweat.

My mother leaned close to the man looming over her, straining to catch his words. She glanced down at me after a minute and realized that I was staring at the white-hot point of light at the end of Big Jack's welding rod.

She grabbed me with a jolt, covering my eyes. "No, no," she said. There was panic in her voice, her nails dug into my arm. "Don't look at Daddy, baby...it'll burn out your eyes and you'll have sand in them tonight."

Very clearly, I remembered lying in bed that night, screaming and crying as my mother held a wet washcloth over my burning eyes.

I dropped the mask with a *clunk* against the floor of the storage room. It folded when it landed, pivoting on the heavy headband. I ran my hands over my face and through my hair, muttering sounds that never quite formed curse words.

When I looked back to the pile, I opened the photo album. The plastic pages were yellow with age. The wax behind the photos had dried and some of them tilted or slipped out as I flipped through it. I held up a picture of my father and me at the hunting lease, posing with our deer. Ricky had taken it while drunk and the whole scene was canted to one side. Until now, I'd forgotten the moment of the photo altogether.

One of my hands rested on the neck of the doe I'd killed. Even removed so far in time, I squinted my eyes and pressed my lips together as I looked at the animal in the photo. My young face was devoid of emotion; the blank expression and the pose gave me the appearance of a mannequin from a hunting store display.

Next to me, my father angled the head of his buck so that it was twisted upright and staring forward. The eyes were flat and black, looking into the camera. Dad held the spiked antlers in each hand and there was an expression of wild enthusiasm on his face in contrast to mine. A chain of some sort hung from his neck, fallen from his t-shirt, and his mouth was open in a grin that evoked the memory of his chuckle. I stared at his face for a long minute before continuing through the album, looking at every photo before setting it aside.

Lastly, I picked up the Ziploc bag containing his wallet. I'd saved it until the end because of the blood. The job of clearing out the storage space was complete, except for this small object.

Reaching into the bag, I took the leather wallet between a thumb and forefinger. It was thick, stuffed with random scraps of paper, identification passes for parts of the plant and membership cards for the organizations to which he'd belonged. It had been in the back pocket of his jeans during the final seconds of his life. Blood had run down from the wound in his head, over the wallet, soaking it. Slowly, I opened the grisly thing, folding it out flat on the floor. Piece by piece, I went through all the ATM slips, scribbled phone numbers, laminated cards and other notes, deciphering all the meaningless words through the meaningful brown stains.

BIG JACK is DEAD

Down in the deepest fold, I found washed-out pictures of Brodie, Ramona, Mincy and me. Holding the curled paper in my hands, I looked over each photo and studied the faces. In most cases, blank expressions looked back at me across the years. Only in one of the pictures was anyone smiling with what appeared to be a genuine expression. It depicted Brodie standing next to a tire swing in the front yard. Wearing nothing but his underwear, he was about five. His hair was still light, as it had been when he was younger, and stood out in cowlicks. I ran my thumb gently over the smooth surface, touching the center of his chest. But his adult face came into my mind, his crazy, pin-point eyes and his slack expression, reminding me of the gulf between us. I shuffled the photos. *Where did my brother go?*

I set the photos down and took everything else out of the wallet. Like a Tarot reader, I spread it out, staring at the pieces, trying to make sense of it all. The copper smell was stronger on the air now. Looking at the arrangement before me, I tried to accept that it had no meaning, no message. Collecting it all from the floor, I threw away the most trivial or bloodstained articles before putting everything else back together in the wallet, including the small photographs.

There was no note.

HARVEY SMITH

I closed doors to the storage unit and paid the bill up front. In the parking lot, I dropped my father's remaining possessions into the trunk of the Lexus and took one last look around, resenting this place for playing a role in my life. Then I drove to the house where my father had killed himself.

Chapter 19

1980

Several days after Big Jack created the ice tree, all but the last of the ice was gone, melted. The tree was ruined. Most of the branches had been snapped by the weight of the ice, the limbs parallel with the ground suffering the worst. Some of the branches reaching upward were still intact and the tree resembled a giant weed. The lawn was a mess, a muddy disaster of tracks and ruts. People from the neighborhood had stopped at all hours of the day to coo over the tree. A miniature mountain range of ice ringed the trunk, standing a foot in height. From the front porch, it looked like a dying ghost, reaching upward in its last gasp, struck down by three days of winter sun.

Jack walked along the sidewalk, returning from Jenny's house. Audible a block away, the garage at his house emitted a metallic screaming sound. When he reached his driveway, he stopped just behind his father's black pickup truck and looked out over the yard in disgust. He held his ears against the noise from the garage. The wreckage of the yard was profound. After he'd taken it in, he approached the garage to see what his father was doing, coming around and settling against the grill of the truck.

Big Jack was busy in his shop, hunched over the oily workbench. His brow was knitted as he studied the object in the vise before him. Under his guidance, a grinder moved in a blur and threw golden sparks up onto the wall behind the bench. The sound of metal being eaten away at high speed was shrill and deafening.

Holding Jack's flashlight, Brodie perched on the workbench. He crouched on one knee among his father's tools and pointed the light down onto the angled metal his father was grinding. Brodie gathered the long, beaded chain, attached to the end of the flashlight, cupping it in his palm to keep it out of the way. A set of pewter deer antlers hung from the chain, resting against the flashlight. He hovered over the vise with a stocking cap balanced on his head. His face very close to the grinder, he wore a protective plastic mask that his father had stolen from the plant.

Moving only his eyes, Big Jack glanced up as Jack approached, scowling when he saw that the boy was covering his ears. Jack lowered his hands.

The light bobbed and Big Jack snapped his attention back to Brodie, bellowing. "You want me to knock you through that wall? Huh?" He cut his eyes back and forth between his youngest son and the grinder. "Hold the goddamn light and don't make me tell you again."

Mincy stood at the kitchen door, bracing it open with her hip. She held a pie pan, clutching it with checkered oven mitts. Steam rose up from the crust. Regarding the scene in the garage with dissatisfaction, she looked to all three of them in turn, irritated that no one had taken significant notice of the pie.

The sound of the grinder dominated everything.

She turned her attention to the younger boy, yelling to be heard over the grinder. "Brodie! Baby, fix your hat."

He called back at her, "What?"

"Fix. Your hat." She screamed this time, cutting through the noise. "It's about to fall off...and it just looks silly hanging down like that."

The last words were drowned out, but the eight year old reached up with one hand to adjust the stocking cap. It stood up from his head ridiculously high and came to a wavy point. He tugged it down into place and the flashlight beam went off target as he did.

Without taking his eyes from the metal he was grinding, Big Jack roared at his son, "Goddammit, boy!"

Startled, Brodie dropped the flashlight into the grinder. The thing exploded, sending the chain, pewter antlers and pieces of the flashlight across the garage and into Jack's face like a cluster of cannon shot.

In an instant, he was thrown back against the truck. He registered three pale faces turn toward him in shock against the backdrop of the dim garage, howling apparitions. Thrashing like a shot animal, his mind went blank and his body flew into convulsions. Brilliant light flared from his left eye and he made no sound for a timeless second. He could not hear and he could not breathe. Only when he began to wail did he realize that he was lying on the concrete under the front of the truck.

They rushed toward him, around him, shrieking like birds fighting over a scrap.

Jack screamed and screamed, but the burning in his face only got worse.

Chapter 20

1999

At the curb, I killed the car and studied the block. Running along the river, it was shorter than most of the streets in Lowfield, oddly truncated. Eight houses sat in a line on the same side of the road. Some of them had sidewalks and some didn't, creating a gap-tooth grin along the front lawns. There were no houses on the opposite side of the street, only a levee, covered in wind-whipped salt grass and pieces of trash. The road terminated at the end of the block in a field of goat weed.

Next to a bus stop, I leaned against the car for a while, unprepared to go into Dad's house. A seagull floated by on an updraft, rising from behind the levee and eying me as it rode the air overhead. I remembered older kids at school bragging about throwing Alka-Seltzer to them during lunch, watching them swoop in to snatch the flat pills, only to fall to the concrete and bleed out minutes later.

I placed my fingertips against my eyelids, holding them closed, pushing against my eyes until I couldn't stand the pressure. "Please," I said to no one.

HARVEY SMITH

There was a bench at the bus stop, sitting on a slab. Someone had hacked "H.B.W." into the wood with a knife or screwdriver and in marker someone had written, "blows his brother" underneath. Off to one side, more graffiti offered a translation, "His Black Wings?" To which someone countered, "Hash, Bitches and Whiskey." Behind the bus stop, a rusted barrel overflowed with garbage and the area reeked. Hunting for a clean spot, I sat down and slumped against the bench.

Masts and antennas were visible beyond the levee, where commercial boats were docked at a decaying marina. When I was growing up, one of my friends had lived a few blocks away and we explored the area often, avoiding drunken shrimpers as they staggered out of the marina bar. Their boats smelled of diesel smoke and dead fish. We often walked to the end of the rotting pier, once a train bridge, throwing bottles as far as we could across the river. The dark waters of the salty river were sheened with prismatic oil and floated with bits of Styrofoam. At the edge of the water, great chunks of rock and concrete sat just below the surface, broken bottles and torn aluminum cans nestled in their mossy crevices like bits of rot in bad teeth.

When I was fifteen, the city attempted to turn the area into some sort of boardwalk. The idea was to hold an event once a month, a fried seafood party with bingo and live music. Along the river, they set up picnic tables and aluminum pavilions. Hoping to draw in people from all over the county, the City Council invited local businesses to set up booths. I went once, riding my bike down to the docks and walking around alone.

It was terrifying…fishermen and day laborers staggering around and yelling. *Hey, kid…you ever had any pussy?* The third time they held the event someone got stabbed to death and that was it. The whole thing was suspended, never revived.

Sitting on the bench, I wondered what my mother was doing. After the funeral had she just gone home to watch television? What had she felt, standing beside the grave? Remorse? Some final sense of freedom? For a moment I felt the desire to call her, to ask, but the notion fled as soon as I remembered what it was like to sit at a table with her, to carry on a conversation. *I visualized her spotted face, but it became Jenny's…older, with blackened teeth and patches of missing hair. She sat in her trailer, a simpering zombie.* Would this have happened if I'd stayed in Lowfield? Would I have hollowed her out just like my father did to my mother?

Leaning back, I looked up into the sky. My mouth tasted like poison. Turning my head, I spat and the saliva tumbled end over end through the air like a boneless acrobat. The wind blew a plastic bag down the street until it got caught under the car.

I made my way up the front walk of the house.

In the neighbor's yard, a rusted bicycle lay on its side, the chain loose and spilled out like entrails. A water-logged football sat next to the bike, the foam torn full of holes like craters. Several bags of trash had been piled around the front steps and one of the bags had been clawed open by a stray dog trying to get at a disposable diaper. I wondered with perverse amusement about what kind of relations my father might have had with the people living around him. A feud? An affair? Either seemed just as likely.

As I approached Dad's front door, a woman came out onto the porch of the neighboring house, calling out across the yard.

"He ain't there." She was in her late twenties, with black hair and pale skin. Bruises ran along her arms and legs. "He killed hisself." She tucked her bathrobe around her body, which might have been appealing a few years ago, but was now lumpy. Just as she spoke, a child peeked out from behind her, hanging onto the pillar of her thick left leg. He wore a diaper, nothing else. Insect bites covered his skin like a constellation of red stars. There was food matted in his baby-soft curls and his mouth was smeared with something that looked like jelly. Probably three years old, he looked across the yard at me with wide eyes.

"He killed hisself," she said again. She was almost smiling, thriving on the words, the most drama-rich part of her week. *I heard her shrieking, falling back as I rushed her, as I forced her backward into her home and choked her to death on the floor while her doomed child watched.*

"Sorry to hear that," I said. "I'm just here to look at the house. I didn't know the man who lived here."

"You movin' in?" She lifted a cigarette to her lips and took a drag. Her other arm lay folded across her waist, holding the robe closed.

I almost laughed at her, thought about smashing her body with the rusted bicycle in her yard. "No," I said. "I work for the owner of the house."

She stared at me, sullen now as I crossed Dad's narrow porch. The child in the diaper scratched violently at the sores on his belly. Reaching down, the woman yanked his hand away.

Looking at the little boy, disgust and sympathy warred across my thoughts. Lowfield was full of his kind, born into a world blighted, following the wake left by their parents, swerving and miserable, only to bring up their own offspring a couple of decades later, often sooner. I turned away, dropping them into an unmarked grave somewhere in my head.

The house was small, maybe 800 square feet. It sat on a plot of land that was barely larger than the house. The porch creaked under my feet. At the far end, away from the front door, I pushed a lawn chair out of the way. Holding one of the pillars supporting the porch roof, I leaned out and looked down the side of the house. A chain link fence ran around the back yard, where I could see pieces of a Frisbee scattered like shrapnel after a blast. Several plastic chew bones protruded from dried mud at odd angles. They reminded me of news footage...cops excavating human remains from an overgrown backyard. *The neighbors never suspected anything. They said he was just a normal guy.* A length of very thick, knotted rope rested in the corner of the yard like a serpent stuffed with newborn kittens. All the grass was gone along the fence and two ceramic dog bowls lay upside down in the dirt.

I peered into my father's bedroom. There were no curtains on the window, but the glass was warped and filthy with dust and streaks. I might as well have been trying to look into another world. The dim space beyond was barely visible, swimming as I shifted.

The front door was unlocked. I tried the handle and pushed the door open. Pausing for a second, I called out into the living room. When no one responded, I entered. The house was quiet and the air inside had a different quality, still and dry.

My father's things were gone of course, the rooms stripped bare. Without furniture, it was bigger inside than I remembered, bigger than it seemed on the outside. The interior smelled like pine-scented cleaning chemicals and I laughed softly, the sound of my laughter surprising me, disturbing the dead atmosphere. *He worked in the plant that created the chemicals. Maybe they used the chemicals to clean up the blood.*

I had visited my father in this place over Christmas just after he moved in. He seemed oddly content. The man was living alone for the first time in his life. He got my mother pregnant when she was a teenager and subsequently he always lived with me, Brodie and his various wives...always with a succession of wives. Living alone in the last days of his life suited him. *That is, until he blew his brains out.*

Visiting for the holidays that year, I was shocked by how much weight he'd lost. This was months before his death and he looked bleached out. The house resembled one of the hunting lodges I remembered from childhood. It smelled of fried bacon, coffee and cigarettes, and it was littered with girly magazines and gun catalogues. Awkwardly, I had presented him with a Christmas gift. Buying gifts for Dad never brought me any joy, but I felt guilty when I failed to do so.

Taking it, he looked concerned. "I didn't get you nothing." He took a slug from his premixed whiskey sour and set the glass down on the kitchen table. Losing so much weight, he looked wiry. Combined with his small stature and his years working outside, he was leathery and elf-like.

"That's okay, Dad."

As soon as I said this, his concern vanished. Ripping into the package, he tore it to shreds and dropped the paper at our feet. He pulled out the t-shirt, which was folded around a card. A stack of gift certificates bulged beneath the front cover of the card; hundreds of pre-paid dollars to the chain stores in the area...cafeterias, a Western-style clothing outlet, an automotive parts shop, a drive-through liquor store. I knew Dad would use them.

The t-shirt depicted two deer, lamenting a target-shaped birthmark circling the eye of one of the deer. Dad had come to mind as soon as I saw the shirt.

He blinked, confused. "I think you got me this same t-shirt last year. Ain't this the same one?"

As soon as he said it, I realized it was true and embarrassment flooded me. "I guess it is," I said. "Sorry...I just forgot. I thought it was funny."

He looked uncomfortable, studying my face with concern before turning his attention to the gift certificates. He draped the t-shirt over a chair at the kitchen table and forgot about it.

"Hot damn, boy. I love the food they got there." He held up the slip from the cafeteria then from the parts store. "...and I need some new tires. I can barely see the goddamn treads." He cocked his head and looked up at me, one eye bulging larger than the other as he broke into a grin, which was the closest he ever came to thanking anyone.

I smiled back at him, but my stupidity nagged me. There was something pathetic about buying him the same t-shirt two years in a row. We just couldn't connect, not even over something as scripted as a Christmas gift. Not over anything.

I stood blinking in the dead air of the house, fighting to pull myself back into the present, back into the world. I walked into the kitchen and looked down at the rickety dinner table, half expecting to see the shirt hanging from a chair.

I saw him sitting there, near the end, drunk and munching on a candy bar, muttering to himself. The lights in the house were off and Dad sat in the dark, lit by the streetlight that fingered in through a kitchen window. I stared across the space, half seeing my father and half seeing an empty room.

All the dishes had been removed from the sink and the cabinets were empty. Someone had made an effort to clean up the counters, but they were so old and scarred that the effort was largely pointless. There were no curtains around the window over the sink. I leaned close and looked out through the screen, filthy with dead insects and spider webs.

The back yard was trashed. Muddy pathways cut back and forth in patterns that only made sense to a dog, orbiting tall tufts of dallisgrass. Leeched of color by the sun, a pale beer can stood half-embedded in a fire ant mound, leaning to the side like a haphazard smokestack. Several lawn chairs were scattered about, one of them on its side. Most of the weaving had rotted away from the aluminum frames and the fringed edges blew in the wind like hair from a dried skull.

I rifled through a couple of empty drawers before drifting

out of the kitchen. Nothing but tiny, pinched mouse droppings.

In the empty bedroom, a spot on the wooden floor had been scrubbed practically white, where the bed must have been. *The cleanest spot indicates the dirtiest deed.* I started to laugh, but the sound caught in my throat.

Kneeling down, I knew this to be the place where my father had finished himself, the exact point in space where Big Jack sat, weeping and raging, cradling his beloved pistol as he rocked back and forth. I touched the floor softly, running my fingers over the old wood. As I traced the outline of the bleached spot, I heard my father speaking in a low tone, next to me. The words were meaningless, unintelligible. He sat there as skinny as a circus freak. I recalled his expressions in life, the way anger, confusion and fear had often moved across his face, as they must have just before pulling the trigger. I wondered what his voice sounded like inside his head. His thoughts, or a caricature of them, spun and fell and floated through my mind like feathers in a dark and empty grain silo.

*****

The pistol on the kitchen table was a Browning BDA,

*manufactured in 1983. Entirely black, it was the snubby
compact model, holding a 7-cartridge magazine loaded with
hollow-point rounds. Like a family of nested dolls, the slugs
were stacked inside the magazine, snug within the grip of
the pistol. The gun rested on a rag streaked with oil, with
the words FABRIQUE NATIONALE HERSTAL visible
along the length of the barrel. On the table nearby, sat a cup
half full of whiskey sour and a coffee mug, speckled with
droplets of blue paint reminiscent of a bird's egg.*

*The house was quiet, with no air conditioning. All the
lights were dark and many of the windows were covered.
Over in the corner, between the ancient refrigerator and the
counter, the floor creaked as Big Jack adjusted his stance.
The joints in his toes cracked as he lifted the heels of his
boots to get a better view out the high kitchen window. In
the dimness of the house, only his face and one hand,
gripping the window ledge, were illuminated. It had been
almost a week since he'd washed or shaved, and his chin and
cheeks bristled with whiskers. His nails tapped on the sill as
he studied the yard.*

*From his vantage point, he could see more of the alley
and the neighbor's yard than his own; sagging chain link
fence, clumps of weed and muddy trails where nothing
grew.*

BIG JACK is DEAD

He shook his head from side to side. Oh, man, he thought, Daddy woulda hated to see that. Just hated it.

At one corner of the yard, a thick rope lay coiled in the mud. He had taken it from a co-worker's fishing boat almost a year earlier, borrowing it for some task he couldn't remember now. He tried to get a glimpse of the dog where it slept against the wall during the day, but he couldn't see it.

At the table, he fell into a chair and took a gulp from the plastic cup. It collapsed under his calloused fingers then popped back into shape as he set it down. When he stopped moving, the house was quiet except for somewhere down the street kids were yelling at one another, their voices faint and brief. Taking up the pistol, he held it in both hands, knuckles yellow-white against the black metal. It was cold, leeching away the heat from his skin. Sighting down the length of his arms, he held the gun away from his body, pointing it at the wall then making a quick correction and aiming at a badly tilted clock hanging five feet off the floor. When he toggled the safety off, the clicking echoed through the old house. The muscles in his arms tensed, ropy and lined with veins. His skin was dark, freckled in places and long-tanned from working outside. A deep sigh escaped him.

He pulled the gun close and flipped it around, closing one eye and straining to see down into the barrel. Swaying a bit, he caught a beam of weak light from the window over the sink, but it wasn't enough to illuminate much of the deep, perfect bore. Looking at the barrel, pistol profile, he contracted his brows and ran his tongue across his teeth, pushing against the enamel. The etched lettering was barely perceptible as his thumb slid back and forth along the surface.

Outside the front door, someone took a couple of heavy steps across the porch. Big Jack jerked his head toward the front of the house, just as a stack of mail shot through the slot in the door, sliding to the floor.

"Goddammit," he said. Caught by surprise, his voice was raspy. Stock still, he listened as the footsteps retreated.

He dropped the pistol onto the cloth and stood. Made with the last packet of mix he had, the whiskey sour was no longer cold, but it lit up his mouth and burned as it went down his throat. Cup in hand, he made his way to the door. In front of the pile, he used the toe of his boot to separate out the mail. He squatted and looked it over, a collage of overdue bills, junk offers and coupon fliers.

A pained expression crossed his face as he picked up one
of the bills, dropped it, and picked up another. He rubbed
his mouth, eyes wide and bloodshot.

A table stood against the wall with a fat county phone
book resting on the lower under-shelf, spine toward the wall
so that the ratty pages faced him. Someone had written his
name, HICKMAN, on the spread of the pages. An old
phone was positioned on top of the table, but the cord had
been yanked from the wall. Grunting, he braced himself on
the table and stood up.

He moved closer to the front door, stepping on the
scattered mail and looking past the edge of the curtain.
Tomorrow was a workday, or he thought it was. It might
have been the middle of June and he winced thinking about
how many days of time-off he'd taken. He tried adding it
up, but couldn't. Whirling in place, he sent envelopes
skittering across the wooden floor, his steps shaking the
house.

Back in the kitchen, he lit a cigarette with trembling
hands and smoked. Squinting his eyes and looking off to the
side, he tried to work it all out. One hand crept through a
wide hole in his t-shirt, fingers clambering along his ribs as
he stared toward the refrigerator. When the compressor
kicked on, it startled him.

HARVEY SMITH

He took a drag and transferred the cigarette to his left hand. Holding it with two fingers, he chewed at the edge of his thumbnail. Eyes still cut to the left, he spat a piece of skin out away from him.

The sun had started to set. Stubbing out the cigarette, he reached for the pack and lit another one. The lighter clinked as he snapped it shut and jammed it into his pocket. The refrigerator shut off again, leaving the house in silence. He reached up and wove his fingers through his hair then pulled hard, rocking in place so that the kitchen chair threatened to buckle.

He tried to say something, but made an urking sound.

Reaching out with his right hand, he clutched at the pistol, dragging the cloth around it and picking up the entire bundle. The weight felt good under his palm. Pushing his chair back from the table, he rose and staggered toward the bedroom.

*****

I realized that our long struggle had ended, that there would be no resolution; none that made sense. My father had made me and then he had unmade himself.

BIG JACK is DEAD

Rubbing my face, I imagined a great nothingness outside the walls of the house, a hissing television on a dead station. It had eaten up the world, causing every single thing to fly apart until nothing was left but a shimmering, buzzing void, dissolving my mother and all the missing pieces of her mind, my lost brother and even the fresh corpse of my father, barely human by my understanding of the word.

I was afraid to go to the window, afraid to open my eyes. Licking my lips, I dropped my hands and stared at the floor, unsure of what to do next.

There was a closet across the bedroom. I walked over, stumbling, and opened the door. There was nothing inside but a roach trap in one corner. I was about to turn away when I noticed a small panel set into one wall, hard to spot in the low light. Stepping inside, I knelt down. The sunlight from the dirty bedroom window was barely strong enough to illuminate the closet. The air was pungent with long-dead animals; mice or opossums under the boards of the floor.

The panel opened with a squeak, revealing a compartment within the wall. Two metal pipes ran behind the ancient sheet rock. There were valves attached to the pipes and a discolored inspection tag hung from one of them. Flipping it over, I saw that it dated back to the 1970's and had been signed by someone named Braeden. My eye caught a small object, something that I recognized instantly. Reaching into the space, I fished it out and looked it over.

Sitting in my palm, the pocketknife was five inches long. The handle was ribbed with black and green rubber. Using my thumb, I snapped it open, exposing the blade that my father kept razor sharp for almost three decades. Stretched across my hand, it flashed in the filmy light creeping over my shoulder. The metal had been discolored by time, with patterns that looked like lakes seen from high above, a prismatic coastline running along their edges. I studied the blade, catching a warped reflection of my own face in the surface. The knife felt good in my hand. How many deer had Dad gutted and skinned with this thing? Over the years the rubber grip had dulled to some unnamed shade of aqua-gray.

I wondered how the knife had come to rest in the small compartment. My father was a practical man, always focused when busy with his hands. Had he been working on the pipes? *I could see him sitting in the closet in the morning light with a cup of coffee on the floor in front of him. I could see him using the knife to cut off the tip of a caulking tube, unfiltered cigarette dangling from his lips, eyes squinted against the smoke.*

BIG JACK is DEAD

A shudder ran through me as I remembered what it was like to be near him while he was working, watching him as he muttered and tinkered. Like I shouldn't exist, a feeling interrupted by overpowering fear during those moments when he needed something that I failed to deliver fast enough or in exactly the right way. I could see his twisted expression, radiating hostility and guilt. *No, boy, the goddamn socket wrench.*

Sitting on the floorboards, I turned the pocketknife over in my hands, depressed the lock and closed it. The pivot was smooth as it clicked shut. I opened and closed it several more times, listening to the sound. The metallic parts were cold, draining the heat from my hand. I tapped the butt of it against the floor a few times, very slowly.

The smell of urine hit my nose, cutting through the antiseptic tang of cleaners and the dusty closet odors. As the air turned rotten, the house creaked and something slapped softly against the floor.

A dark figure stepped into the doorway, blocking the light. He loomed over me, head large. One of his chubby hands reached up and rested on the closet doorframe. In the low light, it took my eyes a second to register the curls, rash of bumps across his pale belly, the low-sagging diaper.

I dropped the knife in surprise and it slid down my body, hitting the floor with a clatter. "Fuck!" My face drew up, lips pulled away from my teeth in a grimace. Half rising, I choked on an intake of breath. The smell from the child's diaper made me want to vomit. He recoiled and his eyes shot wide, huge in his face. Hopping up on one foot then the other, he did a strange little jig.

I stared at him in the darkness, sucking in air through my mouth. When I spoke, my voice was unrecognizable, mewling and strangled. "It's okay. Please...just get out of here. Go home."

Clumsy on his toddler legs, he backed up two steps, pale face dissolving in the dark. Turning, he ran, but fell to the floor before rising and disappearing around the corner. A long wail followed him.

"Goddammit," I said to no one. I almost stood, almost left the house. Instead, I sank back to the floor. The boards beneath me creaked like wooden scaffolding and the wind moaned through the windows of the old place. Exhaustion fell over me like a heavy quilt. With a great sigh, I put my back to the wall, tucking my knees so that I barely occupied any space at all.

Again my eyes settled on the place in the bedroom where my father put the pistol into his mouth. There was a sound and I realized that it was my own voice, that I was laughing. Staring at that clean, clean spot on the floor, I kissed the blade of the knife. The metal felt smooth and cold against the warmth of my lips.

With a fierce motion, I dragged the blade through the meat of my neck. I barely felt the pain and was surprised by the splashing heat of my own blood. A strange relief came over me, something I had never known. Nothing bad could happen. Nothing else, ever again. Noises came from my ruined throat, a voice crying out in a sustained moment of need. There was a great rushing in the darkness around me.

A while later, I took a deep breath and pulled myself up, leaving the knife behind on the floor. My eyes had adjusted to the gloom and when I got back to the kitchen I stopped and took it all in. The quiet, emptiness. There was a shuddering intake of breath over against the wall, then a sniffle. Walking close, I put one hand on the refrigerator and extended the other down to the toddler, who was sitting on the floor. He looked up at me, face slick with snot and tears.

"Hey, hey," I said. "It's all right. I'm not mad." His eyes were locked on mine, searching my face. "Come on, you didn't do anything wrong. I'll take you back to your momma. Okay?"

He gave another involuntary shudder and nodded.

Holding his grubby hand, I stepped out onto the porch, kicking the bottom edge of the door when it got stuck. I wanted to get away, like I'd done something terrible, but I forced myself to walk at his pace. Next door, his mother didn't answer, but he slipped past the screen door and went inside. Partially hidden by the darkness of the house, he stared at me for a few seconds before turning and plodding off to find her.

There was no traffic on the dead end street. The light and the breeze from the levee washed over me standing in the center of the road. Running my hands through my hair, I closed my eyes, listening to the water, the cry of a gull, cars a block or two away.

Pulling out my phone, I called Mandy and told her to get me the earliest flight home. On the plane heading back, I wondered how long it would be before someone moved into Dad's little house. Through the window, into the burning gold of the clouds, there was a trick to the horizon, making it hard to tell whether the sun was coming up or going down.

Deep gratitude to the following readers and allies for their efforts and insights: Leah Smith, Ricardo Bare, Jim Magill, Charles Lieurance, Denise Fulton, David Fugate, Laura Lewin, Stephen Powers, Jane Pinckard, Austin Grossman, Richard Rouse, Debra Ginsberg, David Kalina, Lulu Lamer, Matt Udvari, Bennett Smith, Susan O'Connor, Eric Zimmerman, Michelle Bagur, Monte Martinez, Patricia Maness Nolan, James Teems, Elizabeth Spear, Phil Bache, Anne Spear, Starr Long, Eugenie Long, Jeff Lake, Raphael Colantonio, Florence Colantonio, Kain Shin, Theron Jacobs, Kimberly Whitmer, Tracey Thompson, Angela Ramsey, Laura Ferguson, Jason Rosenstock, Jo Lammert, George Royer, Katie Kizziar, Damien Di Fede, Kristy Bowden, Koley Porter, Brady Dial, Kate de Gennaro, Anthony Huso, Angie Bare, Lauren Magill, Stephanie Whallon, Jeff Lafitte, Anthony Broussard, Jerald Broussard, Brady Fiechter, Sheldon Pacotti, Bruce R. Ladewig, Quin Matteson, Trey Ratcliff, Shay Pierce, Jake Simpson, Seth Shain, Brenda Brathwaite, Joe Houston, Bill Money, Leon Hartwig, Karen Petersen, Rich Wilson, Rita Wagenschein Rosas, Nathan Regener, Brandon Sheffield, Lisa Machac, Brian Sharp, Kris Fregia, Christian Primozich, Kendall Marie Lynch, and Jordan Thomas. Special thanks to Thomas P. Moore and Rebekah Smith for supporting my early efforts.

Printed in Great Britain
by Amazon.co.uk, Ltd.,
Marston Gate.